An Eriskay Love Lilt

Words & Music Kenneth MacLeod and Marjory Kennedy-Fraser

With tender passion

When I'm lone - ly dear white
Thou'rt the mu - sie of my

heart Dark the night or wild the sea, By love's light my foot
heart. Harp of joy, oh cruit mo chridh, Moon of guid - ance by

finds The old path - way to thee. Vair me o _____ ro van
night, Strength and light thou'rt to me. Vair me o _____ ro van

o Vair me o _____ ro van ee Vair me o ru o
o Vair me o _____ ro van ee Vair me o ru o

ho Sad am I with-out thee. _____
ho Sad am I with-out thee. _____

DARK
THE NIGHT
WILD
THE SEA

DARK
THE NIGHT
WILD
THE SEA

Robert McAfee Brown

Westminster John Knox Press
Louisville, Kentucky

Book design by Jennifer K. Cox

First Edition
Published by Westminster John Knox Press
Louisville, Kentucky

This book is printed on acid-free paper that meets the American National Standards Institute Z39.46 standard. ∞

PRINTED IN THE UNITED STATES OF AMERICA
98 99 00 01 02 03 04 05 06 07 — 10 9 8 7 6 5 4 3 2 1

Library of Congress Cataloging-in-Publication Data

Brown, Robert McAfee, 1920–
    Dark the night, wild the sea / Robert McAfee Brown. — 1st ed.
      p.   cm.
    ISBN 0-664-22128-9 (acid-free paper)
    I. Title.
PS3552.R6988D37   1998
813'.54—dc21   98-7944

To

Peter, who led the way up Ben Essie

Mark, who challenged the Wee Folk

Alison, whose voice is the voice of Moragh

Tom, who makes the old art live

*Sydney, who in her inmost being feels the call of the pipes
and to*

*Colin, Akiyoshi, Caitlin, Jordan, Mackenzie, and Riley
along with*

*Betty Van Dusen, whose spirit hovers over all the Hebrides
and*

*Ursula Le Guin, who quite unknowingly and
most generously provided*

The Beginning Place

and is herself a teller of tales

Contents

AUTHOR'S NOTE

I apologize to the inhabitants of Erinsay for inflicting on them a specially designed sheep barge as a means of transporting their cattle from the islands to the mainland. Such a vessel is more a product of my imagination than a reality of their experience.

As the tale unfolds, something strange happens to time and space. There is, to be sure, a major disruption, not to be ignored, between chapters 3 and 4. But there are other disruptions as well: should the harvesting of Moragh's crops precede or follow the equinox? And, pray tell, which equinox? And where is the manse exactly? These are simply reminders that even "ordinary time" and "ordinary space" are not finally under our control.

Moreover, the characters in this novel are not based on any person, living or dead, but are rather my own creation. And I offer a plea to all who read these pages that if you find anything amiss in my presentation of the lore of the isles, you will understand and forgive such mistakes as well-intentioned efforts by one who loves the isles and writes only to share their sustaining and rugged beauty.

Finally, special thanks to Stephanie Egnotovich and Roland Tapp for ongoing encouragement.

Before
Erinsay

It is clear beyond doubt that the arrival of the MacBrayne steamer is the great social event on the island of Erinsay. Anyone not otherwise engaged will be there, just to check on who has purchased anything on the mainland, from sheep-dip to a new carburetor for an old tractor, and to check the size of other parcels that will be delivered next day in person by Callum the Post.

To be sure, those within walking distance gather to see each other, but they are also inspecting those who come to their island on holiday.

The sailing schedule being what it is, any visitor must spend at least two full days between Monday and Thursday, or three days between Thursday and Monday, and folk on holiday usually stay for at least a week if they can afford it. Some have returned for years without number and have staked out their own special territory.

Only a dozen or so get off this time, for the holiday season is virtually over. A few will stay at the hotel, as they have done for years, and the rest will be in farm houses, where the islanders make a few pounds by offering bed and breakfast during the regular holiday season.

First off are three tweedy women who come each year, well-equipped with bird books, walking sticks, and binoculars. As always they have reserved the double room on the harbor side of the hotel, toward which they immediately start walking. Experience tells them that the extra cot will already have been installed, and that tea will be waiting. Who sleeps on the cot is not divulged.

Next come an elderly couple, both unsure of their footing, helping each other down the gangway, gingerly making their way to the van that will take them to the hotel.

There is an Englishman of about thirty, bound to be an Oxford or Cambridge don, who has come either because his subject is Celtic history and he wants to do field research, or because his subject is chemistry and he wants to escape the laboratory for a fortnight.

Two female undergraduates, St. Andrews at a guess, are going to stay together at one of the farms. They are trying not to be caught looking at the Oxford or Cambridge don, though he has been looking at them surreptitiously during most of the three-hour voyage from the mainland. All three are ostensibly watching the island come into view, but the don has already discovered at which farm they are staying, and where it is in relation to the farm in which he has accommodations.

An American couple with four children come off next, overburdened with luggage, the children's excited and strangely accented voices lending a cosmopolitan air to the otherwise provincial scene.

Disembarking last is a single Scots gentleman, who communicates a clear feeling that life has played him false. It is nothing he says or does; he simply walks with the look of a defeated man. Though scarcely thirty, he looks, at this particular moment, much older. His voice, as he asks directions to the home of Hamish Bell, is flat.

Such folk are frequent visitors, men and women who need time to recover from broken love affairs, and others who simply want to breathe slowly and deeply, as they recuperate from the chaotic scramble of life on the mainland. They hike or watch the birds or fish in the freshwater loch, or hire Tammas Brierly to take them in his motor launch to coves otherwise inaccessible on Erinsay's rough coastline. There's a romance such folk have, not only about the Hebrides, but about all the Scottish isles, and they sometimes bring unreasonable expectations for healing, though it is a wonder how the land and sea and sky and wind together so often soothe and recreate.

One such visitor, meaning to pay a compliment, once said to Angus Gunn, "You've a beautiful island. But it's so far away." Angus looked her full in the face, his voice melodious as he asked, very softly, "From where?"

Jamie Stuart was his name, the dispirited one who had asked directions to the Bells' home. Such word soon gets around the island. Once there is a piece of news like a new name, it is known everywhere by nightfall, for on Erinsay, word of mouth is just as fast as telephone, and not so costly. He would be here for some weeks, the message went, beyond the regular holiday season.

But from what he was trying to escape, the message did not say. And he did not seem about to tell them.

The Mainland Now
Jamie Stuart and Annie Cameron

"Jamie Stuart, I'll not be taking that from you."

Annie's manner was defiant and her usually gentle voice was angry. What had started as a difficult but not impossible conversation was rapidly becoming both difficult and impossible.

Annie could sense that Jamie was getting angry. As long as he was in control of a situation, he was urbane, charming, and altogether gracious. But let him begin to lose control, or just as bad, to think he was beginning to lose control, and a frightened look would enter Jamie Stuart's eyes. He was not accustomed to losing, and did not know how to cope with even the possibility of it. He would begin to resemble a cornered animal, wildly looking about for any mode of escape. Since, in addition to his animal instincts, Jamie Stuart also had the gift of speech, he was able not only to embody anger but to articulate it as well. At the moment he was succeeding admirably at both.

And that was a pity, since Jamie was not by nature an ugly man. An ambitious man, to be sure, very successful for one still in his late twenties, he was determined that nothing should impede an even more rapid upward climb.

Which was why Annie's announcement that she was pregnant threatened not only to jeopardize his secure hold on the next rung of the ladder but to jeopardize the very ladder itself. His schedule didn't yet call for marrying and settling down, as he had told Annie repeatedly; there were too many things he had to accomplish before that.

For the present, Abercrombie and Ferguson, Ltd., the dominant architectural firm in Glasgow, must be first, last, and everywhere in between, and until he had reached an invulnerable position within its structure, other things must be postponed. He had grown up in the shadow of Dundee, but even so, his graduation from the University of Glasgow with high honors in architecture had procured for him a good post with a good firm, and he had constructed a well-organized timetable for advancement. Vacation time had been taken at a minimum for the first five years, and was being stored up. He intended that it should remain so at least until he got a leg up over other young aspirants in the firm, particularly one Jock McEwan, an Aberdonian who had had parallel academic achievements as an undergraduate, and was, Jamie conceded with some inner panic, very sharp indeed. In the face of such competition, single-mindedness in professional life ruled out the distractions of marriage, homemaking, and children, which, much as Jamie professed to look forward to them, must be postponed for a few more years.

After some initial resentment, Annie had been understanding, and even proud of Jamie's ambition, and they had finally agreed to what both considered a formal "engagement," or, more accurately, what Annie's parents considered a formal engagement. Jamie's parents did not matter, for both were dead. And Annie believed that Jamie's commitment to her was expressed through his commitment to the advancement of his career. She was content for the moment in her belief that by postponing the wedding, she and the marriage would ultimately reap rewards not otherwise to be procured from the beneficence of Ambercrombie and Ferguson, Ltd.

The arrangement, they both conceded, was not too bad; while they maintained formally separate establishments, they enjoyed a consistent pattern of Saturday nights and Sundays together, with an occasional Tuesday and/or Wednesday night thrown in as well, depending on the pressure at Jamie's office, along with plenty of phone conversations in between.

Jamie's one concession to the other pleasures of the flesh was the fifteen-foot sailboat that he had purchased on time while still an undergraduate, and on which he and Annie occasionally stole away for a Sunday afternoon. He had once sailed all the way down to the Mull of Kintyre, and dreamed of striking out sometime for the Isle of Man, though the latter idea, along with marriage, must of course be fitted into the career advancement schedule.

Jamie was content. He would work late, and arrive early at the office with gigantic amounts of work done, thereby impressing his supervisors and consequently outdoing his peers. By virtue of spartan living he put a good deal into a savings account, and risked only a tiny fixed percentage each month playing the market.

And Annie, on the whole, was content too. Most of all she wanted marriage, she wanted it with Jamie, and she wanted it soon. But she knew he could not be forced. Her job at the law office was hardly exciting—routine was the best that could be said of it—but at least the days were passing, and her bank account was increasing too. And there was always Saturday night (with the occasional Tuesday and/or Wednesday thrown in for good measure) to look forward to.

But there was restlessness in Annie as well. She had a disquieting sense that she was being used, and when the feeling took possession of her, she would once again raise the matter of a wedding date, a matter concerning which Jamie remained consistently evasive.

When Annie had missed her period that April, she had been frightened and had gone immediately to a doctor who prescribed a number of tests at the clinic. As far as the actual tests were concerned, she procrastinated, hoping that temporary emotional distress would prove to be the root of her trouble, and only when the second month had passed did she follow through with tests that unequivocally confirmed her fears.

She had not expected Jamie to be enchanted with news that could only mean an imminent wedding. But she was unprepared for the rapidly escalating aggression that greeted her not-too-confident opener that evening: "Jamie, we've got to change our plans and get married."

"And why would that be?" he asked, expecting either a line of reasoning based on the undesirability of paying rent for two establishments (an argument with which he was familiar and knew how to handle) or else a fresh profession of love, culminating in an assertion that ardor and desirability made longer waiting too painful to be borne (another familiar argument to which he knew how to respond in a variety of ways, not all of them verbal). So he was entirely unprepared for her quiet and definitive, "Jamie, we're going to have a baby."

Jamie's initial reaction was the predictable yet classic male response to news of an unwanted pregnancy: "Are you sure?"

"Of course I'm sure," she responded in justifiable exasperation, "I wouldn't be worrying you for a false alarm. It's three months since I've had a period. And I've been to the clinic and heard from them just today. It is absolutely certain I'm pregnant." To Annie, there was a clear, logical implication to this information, which she proceeded to voice again: "So we must be making wedding plans right away."

Her reiteration of the need for quick and decisive action caused Jamie's urbane, charming, and gracious facade to wilt and then disappear. The concerned animal took over. Jamie looked for somewhere to go, and found nowhere at all. So he responded with the second classic male reaction when confronted with news of an unwanted pregnancy: "Annie, we've been very careful. Things couldn't have gone wrong . . . unless you told me you were prepared when you weren't."

He warmed up to the point, unaware that he was on sinking sand. His demeanor changed. "You've gone and tricked me, have you? You thought, 'I'll get pregnant and then he'll have to marry me right away . . .' "

Annie's usually docile temperament disappeared, and a fighter emerged, the likes of whom Jamie had never seen.

"Jamie Stuart, I'll not be taking that from you! There was no trickery, and you're a filthy man to say so. I wouldn't have slept with you before the marriage except you wanted it so much, and I wouldn't trick you or any man into marriage, and you're a bloody bastard even to think such a thing."

Even as he absorbed her verbal pummeling, Jamie's mind was hard at work. A little surreptitious finger counting made clear that the baby would arrive just as the contracts were to be completed on the seventeen-story skyscraper he was helping to design in competition with Larkin and Peabody, London architects trying to make inroads north of the Tweed. It would be the crucial event of his career thus far, the launching pad to a junior partnership, if he could pull it off. . . . He *must* be available twenty-four hours of the day and night, all through that time, his attention undivided. The distractions of marriage, pregnancy, and a child were simply unthinkable. Even Tuesdays and/or Wednesdays would be out.

He tried diplomacy. "It's no good," he said. "I'm sorry I said what I did. But trickery or not,"—ignoring Annie's bristling—"can't you see that marriage must wait, and we'll simply have to get rid of the baby? For the sake of our futures," he added, to clinch the point.

Diplomacy was unsuccessful.

"Jamie!" Annie was outraged. "I'm not giving up our child, not in a thousand years. You're plain daft if you think so. The baby will be born, and that's flat! Turning to practicalities, "So how do we tell my parents?"

When she received no answer, she took a long breath and continued, "And if you won't marry me, I'll go somewhere else and have the baby by myself. So you needn't speak of trickery any more, Mr. Jamie Stuart." She burst into tears.

The tears heightened Jamie's sense of being trapped. He became a hard-liner.

"You'll bring no child of mine into the world, Annie

Cameron, until it's wanted by the *both* of us." He spoke firmly, getting up and standing over her.

When she sobbed the more, he moved in sheer desperation to the third classic male reaction to news of an unwanted pregnancy: ". . . always assuming, of course," he continued, the angry look now full upon him, "that it *is* a child of mine. You're very sure of that, are you, Annie?"

The sobbing stopped. There was a contemptuous silence, initiated by Annie, who stood up, and with considerable deliberation, slapped Jamie full in the face, drawing blood across his lower lip.

"Oh, so that's the way of it, eh?" Jamie said, grabbing her by the shoulders and shaking her. "Hear me out, Annie. That baby comes out of you good and fast, whoever fathered it—good and fast, you hear? You get to the doctor tomorrow morning!"

And in his anger and fear, he pushed her away—pushed her with all the force of one who has handled a fifteen-foot sailboat in stormy seas off the Mull of Kintyre. Annie, thrust backward, lost her balance. Twisting to right herself, she fell over the rocking chair. It skidded from under her, so that she landed on the floor.

"Oh," she moaned. "You've hurt me, Jamie."

"Nonsense," he shouted, frightened at the power just unleashed in him. He picked her up efficiently but roughly and set her down firmly on the sofa.

"We're in no mood to be talking more tonight," he said. "I'm sorry I pushed you, but your slap was not so friendly either. Now just remember, Annie, one thing is clear: the baby must go. Think on that tonight, and we'll get you to the doctor tomorrow. . . . I'll pay," he added, as if by such an announcement chivalry had reasserted itself and moral order had been restored to the universe.

He left in a confusion of anger, hurt pride, and fear of the potential dissolution of all his dreams, closing the door none too gently, but realizing, even as he did so, that for the sake of appearances to anyone who might be in the hallway, he must not seem to be storming out.

The miscarriage followed a few hours later. Annie knew instinctively that she had lost both her baby and her man. She felt grief at both losses, though the second loss contained a growing measure of anger and bitterness she could scarcely handle. Jamie, she knew, would be relieved rather than saddened by the accident, and she could only feel revulsion toward him for that.

But even more than grief and anger, she felt alone. Alone in the loss of her son (she somehow felt sure it had been a boy), alone in the loss of a lover who had abandoned her in her time of need, and alone in her world, for she had no one with whom she could share these hard realities.

Jamie nursed his own anger and fear, keeping them finely tuned throughout the rest of the evening with the help of an impressive number of libations consumed nonstop at the nearest pub. By morning not only was his head splitting but his psyche was torn in two as well: he was ashamed of himself for his roughness, but he was even more worried that his carefully orchestrated plans for the future might be coming unstuck. He faced two interrelated but mutually exclusive necessities: he must ensure that the baby was aborted, and he must placate Annie for the vigor of his response. The two currents were warring within him. He needed to negotiate a truce.

So late that morning, it being Sunday, he phoned her, still

oscillating slowly increasing remorse for the immediate past and rapidly increasing apprehension for the immediate future.

"Annie . . ." he began as soon as her phone was answered, still groping for how the sentence would end, although fairly sure that remorse would be the best gambit.

He could have saved his worry.

"I'll not be talking to you, Jamie Stuart. There was enough talk last night to last for many a month. Trickery, indeed! But you can rest assured," she almost spat out, "there'll be no wee one. Your shove took care of that."

Jamie's "But Annie . . ." was countered by a loud click.

And then he thought, ah, half the problem is solved; there's no need for an abortion; all that remains is to apologize and patch things up.

He rang back immediately. No answer. He rang back again two minutes later. The phone rang and rang. Finally the ringing stopped. The phone had been taken off the cradle.

But no voice answered his.

"If that's what she wants, that's what she gets for now," was the content of Jamie's interior monologue. "She won't answer the phone? Then the next move is hers."

Five minutes went by, during none of which did Annie make the next move. He called her again. Her phone was still off the cradle. At least, he assumed, that must be the meaning of the mocking busy signal. And then he thought, in a panic devoid of logic, what if she is phoning her parents? Or the police?

He saw the headlines: "Young Architect Arrested in Assault Charge," and so he made his way apprehensively but speedily back to Annie's building. The outside doorbell brought no buzz to let him in. Gaining access by ringing the bell of the super, he ran up to the third floor.

"Annie! Open up. I know you're there."

Silence.

"Annie!" followed by three loud poundings.

No response.

A subsequent staccato of importunate beats succeeded in drawing a response only from Mr. McDougal, the tenant next door, whose Sunday ritual before the television watching the Hotspurs play Edinburgh he had invaded. But no Annie.

"Is it breaking the peace of the Sabbath you'd be about, Mr. Stuart? You'll stop that please, or we'll have the police on you. If your girl is not at home, there's no point knocking any further. And if she is at home, it's clear by now she's not about to let you in."

Jamie could scarcely fault the logic of the argument, and that realization, coupled with old McDougal's threat to call in the law ("Architect's Felony Compounded by Charge of Disturbing the Peace"), was sufficient to force him into humiliating retreat.

Subsequent calls during the next few days were either not answered, or silently terminated as soon as he spoke. Calls to Annie's office number elicited only the information that she was unavailable at the moment and would return his call when convenient. It was never convenient. On Thursday, dialing her number brought on a well-modulated voice advising the caller that the number he was ringing had been disconnected.

Had she gone home? Jamie was forced to call her parents in Kirkcudbright: "Oh, Mrs. Cameron, it's Jamie Stuart here. I was wondering could I speak with Annie?"

"Oh Jamie," her mother responded, "what has been happening? We're very worried about Annie, we are. She came down here two days ago, looking like the devil himself had been after her. All broken up she was, but she wouldn't talk about it"—Jamie breathed an almost audible sigh of of relief— "and we cannot figure out what has happened. Have the two of you had a falling out?"

Jamie professed ignorance of any "falling out." He did acknowledge that there had been a "misunderstanding," though, he suavely assured her, not serious enough to have led to Annie's departure from Glasgow. That point secured, he went on, "Well, where is she now? For I want to go and help if I can, Mrs. Cameron."

"Jamie, it's strange, it is, but she told us we were to tell *no one* where she had gone after she left us, and I guess that includes you too, even though you are her young man, for I'm sure she would have told us if you were to be an exception."

Jamie didn't even bother to argue. He knew from experience that trying to extract information from Mrs. Cameron that she felt was privileged was about as likely as stealing the crown jewels in broad daylight, so after a few concluding amenities he rang off.

And now Jamie Stuart for his part was upset, beyond all accounting of it, a bundle of conflicting fears and feelings. He had assumed that Annie would eventually share his feeling that the miscarriage had been a monumental stroke of luck, even though its circumstances had been unpleasant, and would understand his relief—relief that there would be no child, relief that there would be no hasty wedding, relief that his career would not be jeopardized when the skyscraper plans and bids were under strict surveillance. The quarrel itself had not worried him too much at first—quarrels, he had always found, could be patched up, and once the two of them were reconciled, there would be resumption of the Saturday nights, in due time a wedding, and in due time, again, a baby to take the place of the one just lost. In due time.

But now it began to appear that the reconciliation would not be as swift or as easy as he had thought, and as the days went by, he even began to wonder whether Annie intended that there be reconciliation at all.

Three weeks passed and then there was a letter, postmarked "New Galloway," which he knew to be in Kircudbrightshire, though the first line made plain that the postmark offered no clue to Annie's whereabouts.

Dear Jamie,

I've sent this to my parents to forward on to you. Don't try to find me, for there's nothing more to say between us. If I had not loved you well, it would be easy to patch things up. But what was once so good suddenly became so bad that there's no way I can sort out the one from the other. That you could think me a schemer and a trickster, trying to lure you into a marriage you did not want, and that you could accuse me of lying with another man once I'd given myself to you—those are not things on which I'll build a marriage. So I'm asking you not to seek me out when I go back to Glasgow.

It's grieving I am, and betrayed I feel, not only for the two of us but for the wee bairn that was the fruit of a love I thought was good and pure. But I'll think no more of it, nor best had you.

Annie

The word "love" seemed to have been written on the line above the word "Annie," inscribed there by force of habit, but it had been smudged out.

Now it was Jamie's turn to grieve, and grieve he did, even a bit for the loss of the child he now thought of as *their* child, but mostly for the loss of Annie. It was something new to discover that she was no longer on the other end of the phone when he felt lonely, nor there on Saturday night when he felt loving, nor there on Tuesday and/or Wednesday when he felt both lonely and loving. Having lost Annie before he realized quite how precious she was to him, having taken her presence and her love so much for granted, he became aware for the first time that there were things besides his career that mattered to him, and that now he had lost them. The thought of a career without Annie in the midst of it left him increasingly disconsolate.

What good were the triumphs without someone with whom to share them? What were the weekends worth, if spent alone? What use would the burgeoning savings account be, if there was no one with whom to plan its expenditure? What was the point of all the hard work, the extra hours, the self-denial, if they were not the building blocks for a future shared with her? Why dream about a seventeen-story skyscraper, when the dream most worth dreaming had within it the face of a woman who receded with each successive dream, or, when vividly present, was more distant than ever once the dream ended?

Jamie still got to the office early and stayed late, and with no diversion whatever, threw himself unreservedly into his work, still consumed by a desire to score a coup with the skyscraper plans and then offer the news of a junior partnership to Annie as a bid for reconciliation.

The weekends were a problem. He tried at first to bring extra work home, but the repetitive sameness of his life left him more frustrated and disconsolate than ever. Saturdays were a nightmare to be lived through by deliberately courting oblivion

through enormous drinking binges that would render him co-
matose until late Sunday afternoon. Once or twice a woman,
picked up at a bar, turned up alongside him in bed, but she
would be gone by the time he became fully conscious. Usually
there was just a long solitary chunk of time, endured until the
workweek could absorb his energies . . . until the next Friday
night and a repetition of the whole process.

Soon the work held his interest only until Thursday
night. And then only till Wednesday noon. No more the occasional Wednesday night interlude that had previously
been available with Annie. One Monday he woke up posi-
tively dreading to go to work. He realized he was not only
bored but alienated. It came to him with all the clarity of
Monday morning sobriety that his talents were being exploited. It came to him that other people were deciding how
he should use his time. That he should really have been an
artist. That he was in a rut.

It came to him, poignantly, that he missed Annie. Efforts
to reestablish contact with her were futile. He had tracked
down a new address and phone number for her, and one Sunday afternoon he rang her up. A man's voice answered. He
slammed the phone down, frustrated at having dialed a wrong
number. He was halfway through redialing before paralysis
overtook him: perhaps it wasn't a wrong number.

Paralysis remained. He could not face finding out.

That Monday he was late for work.

Tuesday he forgot an appointment.

Wednesday morning he snapped at a client.

Wednesday afternoon he threatened to fire his secretary.

Wednesday evening he was up until 3 A.M. finishing the
floor plans of a proposed office remodeling job in Ayr that he
had forgotten was due on Thursday.

Thursday morning the client from Ayr appeared right on schedule and was gratified to inspect the completed drawings but puzzled that the proposed renovation included no bathrooms.

Thursday afternoon Jamie lost his cool in a conference session with Mr. Ferguson and several others, accusing Malcolm McDonald of having pirated two of his ideas and incorporated them unacknowledged into the Linzee project on which bids were about to go out.

Friday morning he was obliged to send Mr. Ferguson a memo acknowledging that specifications for the Chisholm Primary School, due that day, could not possibly be completed for another fortnight.

Friday afternoon he found a note in his office box neither requesting nor suggesting but simply announcing that Mr. Ferguson would see him Monday next at nine sharp.

Old Ferguson followed his long-standing policy of starting with the good news rather than the bad news.

"Mr. Stuart, I don't mind telling you that you've made a good record with the firm of Abercrombie and Ferguson, and we've had you marked for a fine future."

Jamie, who had entered the inner sanctum of the second of the senior partners unaware of the long-standing policy, inwardly relaxed.

"Why thank you, sir," he said, smiling and beginning to unwind. Perhaps there had been a reprieve.

Mr. Ferguson again took charge, this time more sternly.

"But I feel minded to tell you, Mr. Stuart, I haven't been feeling that way these past weeks, nor," he continued, following with a coup de grace, "has Mr. Abercrombie. You are not so prompt for meetings. Your drafts are late. Your designs are ordinary, and on top of all that, you've been beating down unmercifully on the clerical staff. So I'm asking you, Mr. Stuart, what is the trouble? Are you in over your head? Can you not do the tasks we assign you? Should we give some of your work to Jock McEwan? It's no way to run a company, I need not be telling you, Mr. Stuart, when folks like you are not pulling their full weight. What have you to say for yourself, Mr. Stuart?"

Jamie found the power of speech difficult to summon after such a barrage, and the possibility of his salvaging himself was close to nil. He was not about to confide to one of the heads of the firm, "I've broken up with my girl," and since that was the real reason for his increasing ineffectiveness at the workplace, his stumbling attempts at explanation communicated nothing to which Mr. Ferguson could relate.

After five minutes in which Jamie's ineffectual stammerings left the situation considerably worse than before, Mr. Ferguson took charge again.

"All right, Mr. Stuart," he commenced, speaking slowly and precisely, "either you don't know what the trouble is, which is not so good, or you do know and choose not to say, which is your privilege of course, but is also not so good, since either way it's clear that whatever the trouble is," he paused, looking over the top of his horn-rimmed glasses at a cowering Jamie," it is affecting your work for the firm adversely. Very adversely," he concluded, after which he indulged in a considerable pause in case the message had not sunk in.

Then, more briskly: "Now Mr. Stuart, in this kind of situation, which, I must say, we've faced before in the firm, I've got three choices, and over the years I've exercised them all.

"First, and simplest, I could fire you." Jamie flinched. "But we've invested a lot in you and don't yet wish to mark you off as a bad debt. So I'm not going to do that, at least not yet.

"Second, I could put you on notice, something like 'Get ahold of yourself, Mr. Stuart, and do it quickly, for the firm is not about to let you do a mediocre job and besmirch our name, nor are we prepared to squander our money paying for work you don't produce.' I'm not going to do that just yet either, though we may come to it, I warn you, for I'm not sure it will work, considering the state you've already worked yourself into."

Jamie, silent, wondered that alternative was left.

"There's a third course, Mr. Stuart. I haven't done it many times, and it's not soft I am, but for the good of the firm I propose it. It is to say, 'Mr. Stuart, we want you with the firm, and we want you with the firm thirty years from now. You're in some kind of trouble now. What can we do that's best for you *and the firm?*'" He emphasized the last words. "And while I never did go much myself for the psychiatry business, I do know that a real change of scene can sometimes work wonders. Mr. Abercrombie and I think it's a good investment to give you some time off to get things sorted out. I've been checking your record, Mr. Stuart, and you've got considerable accumulated holiday leave you've not yet used. We appreciate your sense of devotion to the firm, but it isn't working, Mr. Stuart. And though we're busy just now, we're always busy, and since we've weathered crises in the past without you, we can probably weather one or two more without you."

Mr. Ferguson paused for a moment, almost smiling at what he considered to be a witticism, or at least a nice turn of phrase.

"So what I'm proposing, Mr. Stuart, for the sake of your future value to the firm, is that you take what holiday time is already coming to you, which amounts," he consulted a sheet of paper, "to forty-seven days, and add on to it another fortnight, so you can get a full change of scene, and see if you can't get things put back together."

After this beneficent offer, sternness returned to Mr. Ferguson's face and manner, and certain fiscal matters were immediately attended to. "You'd best know, Mr. Stuart, that the time beyond your forty-seven days of holiday is at your own expense. We'll not be managing that extra time, but we'll see you through the forty-seven days of holiday you have coming to you, and then put you on leave without pay until you return. At which time, Mr. Stuart," said very slowly, "we'll expect you to be fully sharp again."

The brisk manner returned. "Now then, Mr. Stuart," he queried, reaching for pen and paper so that he could record the answer, "just so we'll know how to get in touch with you, where would you be planning to spend your holiday?"

Jamie, to whom the very idea of a holiday had been foreign territory as little as ten minutes ago, was not yet ready to share a complete travel itinerary. In fact, he was not the least bit pleased with the idea. Surely in forty-seven days plus another fortnight, every rational fiber of his being told him, Jock McEwan would have outdistanced him irretrievably in the struggle up the ladder, and Jamie would be doomed to a junior position for the rest of his life.

He was clearing his throat, preparing to suggest that the whole idea was off the wall, when he remembered (in what was probably the first prompting of divine guidance Jamie Stuart had ever experienced) that since it had been Mr. Ferguson's idea in the first place, a vote of no confidence in Mr. Ferguson's idea could only be viewed by that gentleman as a vote of no confidence in Mr. Ferguson. Such a conversational route, quickly surveyed by Jamie, was even more quickly abandoned during a single throat-clearing.

He weighted a number of holiday possibilities, none of them exciting or conclusive. But as Mr. Ferguson was already exhibiting impatience at this latest example of his employee's indecisiveness, Jamie concluded that any words would be better than none.

"I've always had a yen to visit the islands, Mr. Ferguson," he began, "Barra or Jura or Erinsay or . . ."

"Ah!" responded Mr. Ferguson, quick on the uptake, "Erinsay! An excellent choice, Mr. Stuart, an excellent choice. Now it so happens I know the minister on Erinsay and I'll just write him . . ." and then as Jamie looked genuinely alarmed at the thought of any sort of liaison with clerical types, ". . . you need not worry, Mr. Stuart, he'll not be out to convert you, though it might not be a bad idea considering the present state of your soul. But he and his wife—Hamish Bell it is, and Jennie—have an old manse, and they have in a few boarders during the holiday to supplement the stipend, which I gather on the islands is none too fancy. I'll write him directly and see whether you could stay for a spell now the season is almost over. Their rates are reasonable, Mr. Stuart, you can depend on it."

Jamie sat silent. Never before had events slipped so rapidly, and so irretrievably, out of his control.

"That'll be all, Mr. Stuart," was the exit cue Mr. Ferguson furnished him, looking up from his desk a moment later and finding his employee still there. "I'll let you know the moment I hear from Hamish. In the meantime, just so you're keeping your hand in, suppose you get that Chisholm project tidied up, eh, Mr. Stuart?"

Jamie took an awkward leave of Mr. Ferguson, whose

attention was already focused on an estimate of the cost of concrete pilings for a loading platform being designed for construction in the Gorbals. The estimates must have been in order, for by the time Jamie had returned from a short trip to the "gents," he heard Mr. Ferguson saying, "Miss McIntosh, will you take a letter please, to the Reverend Hamish Bell, The Manse, Erinsay, Argyll, Dear Hamish."

Any elation he might have felt over the prospective of new experiences opening up was more than counterbalanced by the realization that he had been manipulated, and that there was absolutely nothing he could do about it.

The Island Now
Duncan MacDuff

No matter that he had been on Erinsay thirty-two years and would be there until he died, Hamish Bell, pastor of the kirk, was an Outsider, a mainlander. No matter that the island itself had not produced a candidate for ordination in the kirk in the twenty years before Hamish came, so that, after the death of his predecessor at the age of ninety-two, it was Outsider or nothing. No matter how hard Hamish tried, there was still a gap he would never fully overcome, a lingering suspicion on the part of the islanders that a mainlander could never truly understand their life and ways, their fears and hopes.

There was another side of it, of course, which had nothing to do with where Hamish had had the misfortune not to be born, but inherent in the fact that, from the perspective of the islanders, Hamish didn't really "work." True, he toiled manfully in a garden in the recalcitrant soil behind the manse, and there had been a disastrous attempt to raise a goat. But he did not tend sheep, or pilot a fishing boat, or mend fences, or have a shop, or milk cows. Which is to say, once again, that he didn't really "work." And the slightly portly body Hamish carried around did nothing to dispel the vocational distance between himself and the lean, hardy, weather-beaten males whose mothers had had the good sense to birth them on Erinsay.

After some initial resentment over being perceived this way, Hamish had accepted it in good humor as a fact of life—something as intractable as sin, and just as unlikely to be overcome this side of the return of the Son of God in glory.

He and his bride had settled into the comfortably roomy, if drafty, manse, built in a time of greater affluence on the island. He had raised two sons, Alan and Bruce, both of whom, when they left for university, made clear that they would not return to the island, save for periodic family visits. Both had honored their intentions by settling, respectively, in Aberdeen and Blairgowrie, schoolteachers if not kirk teachers, and they did bring their children each summer during holiday for a fortnight's visit. It was their recent departure, the week before Jamie's arrival, that had opened up room for Jamie to enter the manse as a boarder.

Hamish's wife, Jean, or, as local custom had long since rebaptized her, Jennie, was not only a mainlander, but a lowlander to boot, having been born in Dumfries, perilously close to the English border, and there were some who went so far as to say that way back in her ancestry there had been English blood. And yet despite this awesome if unverified handicap, she had in some ways adapted to island living more readily and fully than her husband. Jennie had gone part way through a nurse's training program at Glasgow before meeting Hamish, and although their marriage and his subsequent call to Erinsay had foreclosed her finishing the course, even the partial training she had gotten put her far ahead of most of the islanders in terms of diagnostic skills. In commonsense areas of medical wisdom, particularly in relation to herbal medicines, she had from the start deferred to the folk-wisdom of the women of Erinsay. But when matters became complex, she would be drawn in, and her presence at most birthings, prolonged illnesses, diseases, and deathbeds was evidence that she surely ministered to the islands as fully and effectively as her husband. She could hold her tongue as well, so all kinds of island gossip were safe within her mind and heart, sifted and stored there, not for malicious purposes but as possible material for later healings of soul and body, when a word of counsel was either sought from her or offered by her.

Hamish, recipient of a call from God in his teens, single-mindedly pursued sacred literature at the university, and had just completed training when the "living" on Erinsay fell vacant. He had been initially attracted by a somewhat romantic view of Hebridean existence, a factor that his tender Calvinist conscience successfully suppressed, since he had never quite shed the ancient Presbyterian article of faith that if a thing was pleasurable it must be wrong. More practically, he had hoped that the relatively untrammeled pace of island living would enable him to complete a dissertation on the concept of grace in the Pauline epistle to the Romans, which would lead to a university chair in biblical literature.

Both the completion of the dissertation and the dream of a

scholarly life had been indefinitely deferred by the rugged realities of existence on a Scottish island and a greater round of parish duties than he had expected. He had realized, perhaps five years along the way, that he was unlikely to receive a call back to a mainland parish, and that his whole professional life was destined to be spent on Erinsay. By the time the perception was clear, he had consented to it, having persuaded himself that both destiny and the hand of God were at work in all such things.

Hamish was not a strict Calvinist, which means that he took a generous view of God's mercy instead of a rigid view of God's judgment. He had decided, as soon as his theological learning began to be tempered by human relationships, that it was not his task to determine the fate of those who died outside the protective arms of the kirk. It was even quietly rumored among a few folk that he held to a belief that Baptists as well as Presbyterians could be saved, though a matter of such high import and potential scandal never became a matter of public speculation.

Jamie Stuart settled in comfortably with the Bells. The large front room upstairs was at his disposal and he had total independence of movement, save for evening mealtime, the time of which was as unyielding as the laws of the Medes and Persians. He could get up in the morning whenever he liked, warm up the already-cooked porridge, brew a new pot of tea, and then take off on a hike, carrying enough food in a knapsack to tide him through until the command performance at 7 P.M. in the dining room, just after the evening news on the BBC. That left at least an hour and a half of daylight after the meal was done, which was usually spent climbing the mountain known as The Rise to watch the sunset, and dropping in at the pub for a quick one before closing time.

True to Mr. Ferguson's promise, Hamish made no attempt to prod Jamie into kirk activities, though as a courtesy Jamie decided to attend each Sabbath morning and sit with Jennie. The Bells gave him free rein of their house and garden and did not pry into his past or the reasons for his extended stay, though Jamie intuited early on that if he ever needed to talk about such things, Jennie could be counted on both to listen well and be sparing in her "advice."

Jamie was perceived by the islanders, from the moment he came down the gangway of the MacBrayne steamer, as one who had gone through either a business reverse or a divorce, and therefore in need of the slow healing that the clean air, glistening beaches, and springy sod of Erinsay could some-times supply. When he volunteered no information beyond the comment that he was on "an extended holiday," the island folk respected his reticence, and although they speculated at length behind his back, their courtesy was such that they made no frontal assaults upon his privacy.

The one rule of conduct Jamie had brought with him to Erinsay was "don't push," which, when examined, obviously meant: don't try to insinuate your way into other lives, don't ask nosey questions, and above all, don't gossip. There was a "law" on Erinsay, a law never articulated in so many words but clear nonetheless, and as applied to Jamie it went: if you, as a mainlander, hear gossip, it is a sign that you are trusted; but if you, as a mainlander, repeat gossip, it is a sign that you have betrayed trust. Repeating gossip was a perquisite reserved for the islanders.

So Jamie roamed the hills, and watched the gulls, and met the boat, and visited the pub, and went to the kirk, and became a familiar figure in parts of the island within a close enough hiking distance to the manse to ensure a return by seven sharp each evening. He would now and then be asked in for a cup of tea when he stopped to ask directions, and so he began to ask directions more and more. If he did not stop thinking about Annie, at least he found himself thinking about other things as well.

Jamie gradually discovered that as far as the isle of Erinsay was concerned, there were not only two villages, Erinsay to the east and Mulgarry to the west, but virtually two islands. For down the middle of Erinsay, running roughly north and south, ran a prickly spine, a range of mountains—*bens* they were called—that were fierce and steep on the eastern side, but gently sloping to the sea on the far, or western, side, where there was arable land and good farming, as well as plenty of room for sheep. The climate on the far side was milder through the winter, due to the presence of the Gulf Stream, which passed not too far from the shore, even though when a winter storm swept in, it was bitter cold.

Although Jamie had not yet gotten over to the Other Side of the island, as it was invariably called among the folk he had gotten to know, he marveled at the fact that the more rugged and inhospitable eastern side of the island ("*This* Side") was more fully populated. He initially attributed the fact to a further Presbyterian propensity to view comfort as one of the most efficient snares of the devil, and would have continued in this mistaken notion had not Hamish supplied a more mundane reason: the western coast had no harbor, so that any contact with the outside world was afforded only from the navigable bays and inlets to the east.

The difficulty of traversing the road over the mountains contributed to the infrequent contact between inhabitants of the two villages. Because of the steepness of the bens on the east side, the connecting road was a narrow, unpaved succession of switchbacks, a nightmare after a rainstorm, particularly in pony and cart, which was about the only civilized way it could be negotiated. Shortly after its construction, the islanders, in an exercise of understatement, had nicknamed it the Rutted Road, and at all times and in all places the name sufficed. There still, deep in the bowels of the judiciary systems, was a case demanding relief from the "malfeasance in public office" of those who had essayed to construct the road, occasionally exhumed for trial, but nothing had ever come of it. Except for Hamish, Callum the Post was the only one foolhardy enough to traverse it regularly in a motorized vehicle, and that was only because it was the solemn sworn obligation of an employee of the Royal Mail to make the journey to the Other Side of the island on at least the two days each week following the arrival of the boat from Oban to distribute the letters, magazines, catalogues, and sheep serum that had just arrived.

Historically, therefore, there had been a lack of ongoing interchange between the two sides of the island. There was little rivalry, no hostility, much remoteness. Sometimes for an evening of songs and stories (a *ceildh*) or a wedding or a sheepshearing, the two villages would renew acquaintance for the span of a day or two, but long weeks and even months would intervene between such events. In the little village of Mulgarry on the far side there was a tiny school and a tinier shop that did more business with its pub than with its other merchandise, and every other week, on a Sabbath afternoon, Hamish would make the trek over the Rutted Road in his ancient Austin to hold services in a tiny chapel that had been built on the edge of town in an age of more robust faith. In latter years (an age of declining faith, if Sabbath attendance was a reliable index) a gathering of eight hardy souls on such occasions would be festive reinforcement to Hamish, who sometimes had to take what comfort he could from the scriptural promise that when two or three were gathered together the Lord would be in their midst.

Sometime, Jamie kept reminding himself, he must hike to the Other Side of the island, but there was so much left to explore on the eastern side he as yet had felt no great compulsion to wander farther afield. As a result, he knew nothing of the McGuffies or the Gillies or the McCallums or the Langes or the two dozen or so other families who populated Mulgarry and environs.

That came to pass only after the time of his great astonishment—when, in dire straits, he attempted to drink himself into oblivion and found that the cure worked only for a brief time.

One rainy night, when there was no sunset and therefore no point to climbing The Rise, Jamie wound up at the pub long before closing time, with an opportunity for considerably more than just a quick one. After a discouraging twenty minutes of total neglect by the other patrons, he proposed to the host that the next round for the house was on him. He was duly rewarded by an invitation to move over to the large circular table where conversation was already loudly proceeding, and stories were beginning to compete with one another.

Jamie was just comfortably seated when old Tammas Brierly, corncob clenched between his teeth, recaptured the drift of a conversation so happily interrupted by Jamie's act of enlightened generosity.

"Aye," Tammas continued, "and that reminds me of the tale of Padraic McQueague, rest his Catholic soul in peace. Have I ever told you about Padriac's walk home one night from this very pub well on sixty years ago?"

"Never," the remaining eight of them lied in unison, knowing the tale almost as well as Tammas.

After an elaborate clearing of his throat without once removing the pipe from his mouth (an achievement at which Jamie marveled), old Tam continued:

"Well now, Padraic—who, of course, was part Irish, being descended from one of the families that came from Erin long ago and gave our isle its name—Padraic tells how just before his marriage and shortly after the electricity first came to the island, he was walking home alone from here late of a Friday night, and went past the ruins of the tiny grave that, as you recall, legends tell us is the burial place of Saint Elfred, one of the followers of Saint Columba, back fifteen hundred years ago."

Turning to Jamie to clear up whatever references might seem obscure to an outsider who had been so thoughtful as to provide a pint apiece on the house, Tammas explained, "Elfred was hacked to pieces for trying to bring Christianity to the island. After his murder, a two-headed calf was born in the cow barn of Ruaric Ruarich, leader of the killers. Now this was known to be a sign of the evil eye, so Ruaric and the others confessed their crime, built a cairn on the spot of the murder, knelt down, and professed the faith of Elfred. It has ever since been a holy spot on Erinsay, though not so much, I dare say, since the time of John Knox and the triumph of the Protestant Reformation."

Tammas was a loyal member of the kirk session and would brook no nonsense from papists.

"Well, late that night," Tammas continued, turning back to

the rest of the group and the original story, "as Padriac was walking by the place—keeping his distance, to be sure—he saw that the grave was all bathed in light, and marveled that the electricity had been brought to the island not only for the cow barns and farmhouses, but to brighten up a sacred shrine as well. . . . Which was all very fine," Tammas went on, "save that when Padraic went by again in the full light of day, he noticed a very strange thing: there were no wires leading toward the cairn, and there was no pole or spotlight or any means whatever," and Tammas paused dramatically, "by which the electricity could have lighted up the spot. A miracle, by all that's holy!"

"Now Padraic," Tammas editorialized, "as has been remarked by more than one, was part Irish and we Scots know how the Irish are with a tale, particularly when there's been a bit of celebrating beforehand, which in the case of Padraic McQueague was more than likely. But for fifty years he stuck to his story that there had been a holy light from heaven, and scarcely added a thing in all that time, save that in the later years he was sure that there had been angel music in the air above the grave as well."

Turning again to Jamie, Tammas reported in a burst of conspiratorial frankness, "We Protestants have had no dealings with angels on the island, but that it might have been the Wee Folk singing—it being a Friday and all, and the air so 'thin'—ah, that's not so hard even for the rest of us to believe."

Fourteen nodding heads around the table indicated to Jamie that Tammas had just articulated a widely held consensus.

It was not so much the story itself as it was the multiple nods of corroboration at the end of the story that convinced Jamie that there were some things he should check out with Hamish.

Were they corporately pulling his leg? Or did they really believe such tales? Jamie reasoned that Hamish, as an Outsider himself, might have a more disinterested stance toward the local lore than his drinking companions, and could be questioned without being affronted. That the men in the pub took talk about Wee Folk seriously, Jamie attributed in part of the superior qualities of the malt liquor he himself had provided them. But he could not gainsay the fact that he had heard quite matter-of-fact talk about Wee Folk in many of his other island conversations, and reports of their doings were frequently made in conjunction with a description of the atmosphere of the island as "thin," a word Tammas had also used.

But Hamish was off on a sick call the next morning by the time Jamie appeared in the kitchen, and so Jamie settled in for a brief go at *Erinsay: Past and Present,* a huge tome by W. E. G. Sheppherd, B.A., B.D., M.A. (honors), usually kept behind the glass door of the living room bookcase.

Professor Sheppherd, with uncommon grace, had given a first and comforting place in the preface to the comments of Betty Bartholemew, a convert to the island ways:

"In spite of the raids and battles and slaughterings that took place, the peace of the sanctuary still hangs over it . . . I can imagine no more fragrant turf under which bones might rest then that provided by the flower-spread grassy meadow . . . as a quilt. The very spirit of peace broods over it. And at night, when the song of the birds is stilled, above the wash of the waves, the song of the seals is heard, faint yet persistent, singing two alternating notes."

By the next paragraph, however, Professor Sheppherd himself had taken over:

"The past hangs heavy over Erinsay. It's a rich history we have, full of saints and villains, invaders and settlers, fierce battles and peaceful valleys, a coastline dotted with glistening beaches and stern cliffs, surrounded by a sea blue beyond belief, that has alternately been churned white by a storm and turned incarnadine by the blood of Vikings, Danes, and Norsemen doing battle with Picts and Celts.

"The atmosphere we call 'thin' is a line between present and past, between the robust world of our rocks, hills, beaches, sheep, and wild goats, and the spirit world that broods over it—and that line is, as more than one will say, 'very thin indeed.' One can step through it, or across it, or (as a few say) be summoned across it without willing it.

"There are those to this day who claim to have seen invaders coming toward the beach in strange boats like those now seen only in museums on the mainland, waving ancient swords and wearing leather tunics over crude chain mail, emitting gutteral shouts, invading hordes who vanish only when the viewer screams in terror and then feels foolish to have recoiled from those spirits of another age."

There was more in a similar vein, and although it provided Jamie with information, it did little to reassure him that the folk of Erinsay were part of his own twentieth-century world of elevators, computers, cost-benefit analysis, atomic weapons, and association football. To him, all such things seemed incompatible with Wee Folk singing in the air or invading armies a thousand years off schedule vanishing at the sound of a single scream.

If one world was real and the other fantasy, Jamie Stuart would have had no difficulty casting his vote for reality.

He tackled Hamish that evening after supper. How, in this day and age, he wondered aloud, could folk take such matters seriously?

Hamish warmed up to the discussion anecdotally.

"There are loads of tales and legends on Erinsay," he mused, lighting his pipe, as he always did, with all the deliberation born of decades of experience, "and most of them have to do with the atmosphere being, as they say . . . ," he corrected himself, smiling, "as *we* say, very 'thin.' They tell on Iona, which is the truly holy spot of the Hebrides, that a worshiper in the cathedral there will sometimes see an old Druid, dressed in ancient armor, standing by the communion rail, brandishing a sword, to keep the worshipers away from the altar. The first time this happens, the worshiper is fair surprised, as is not to be wondered at, and there's more than one who will remark on it afterwards, but having heard the tale so many times, the pastor at Iona will respond, 'Ah yes! it happens frequently,' which leaves the guest more bewildered than ever. But the pastor then goes on to explain, 'Before the Benedictines built this house of worship, the site was a place of Druid sacrifice, and they still resent the way we Christians took over their place of worship. The old Druids agitate the most just before we celebrate the Holy Supper.'"

Hamish paused at this point in the recital, not sure just how much he should or should not presume about Jamie's previous indoctrination in things eucharistic. Feeling, and rightly, that the latter comment might not be self-explanatory to Jamie, Hamish digressed: "We teach that the once-for-all sacrifice of Christ has made it unnecessary to repeat sacrifices any more. But the Druids look on that as a desecration of their altar of death, on which new sacrifices must continually be offered to their gods.

"Not that I've ever seen such things myself as ancient Druids," Hamish added quickly, "but it's a fact that more than one has claimed to see that old Druid guardian in the chancel at Iona, and, strangely enough, their descriptions of what he looks like always tally.

"But you were not asking about Iona but about our own Erinsay," he continued, half in apology for going so far afield. "I don't believe our kirk is built on a sacred spot of Druids or Picts and Celts. But there *are* spots on the island that the elders will tell you are inhabited by the Wee Folk. I don't believe in the faeries myself, of course—it's against my religion—but a fair number will tell you they've heard faery music on Friday nights before the green mounds."

"The green mounds?" Jamie queried. It was not so much an interruption as an invitation to continue.

"But wait a minute, laddie, don't run on ahead. If you want to know more about such matters, the one to see is Duncan MacDuff. Folks all say his pipes have mysterious power, and I for one would be ready to believe it, so strong they are when he's blowing them on a hillside late of an afternoon. He works hard and he plays hard, does Duncan, so you'll have a better chance of talking to him of an evening in the pub than during the day down at his farm. As for the Sabbath, I'm afraid you'll not find him in the kirk, for there is one piece of scripture that Duncan takes with absolute seriousness, and that is that the Sabbath is a day of rest."

Duncan MacDuff. Having seen him only from a distance, Jamie nevertheless knew that here was a man to be reckoned with, from his very name to the power of his pipes. In the islands they still say a person's name with care, whereas on the mainland folks are sometimes careless, rushing along at a foolish pace in order to get things done. In Glasgow, a name like his would often come out abruptly as "*Dunk*'n," rushed over quickly, whereas on the island it is savored and lingered over. "*Dunn*-c'nn," it becomes, the "n's" being held onto by the tongue on the roof of the mouth for their full measure and then some, before being regretfully relinquished.

So the name was soft and gentle, and so with one side of his being was Duncan MacDuff himself. A huge, strong man he was, as one look at him would testify, but also soft and gentle, especially in the way of his hands, whether in the shearing or the lambing, and he was a master of both. He could wrestle a huge ram to the ground in order to cut the wool, and then shear him with never so much as a nick to the skin, and he could bring forth a tiny lamb out of the mother's body when the cord was twisted, as gentle and tender as ever a woman could be, and then cradle it in one arm, while with the other arm he would fight off the gulls that always swoop around on such occasions to peck at the eyes of the one just birthed.

But when he played the pipes . . . ah, then Duncan Mac-Duff was not gentle, nor was he soft. For "soft" is not a word for the pipes or one who plays them—unless you're a long way off, perhaps three hillsides away. Then the music is gentle and beseeching, and there are those who at the sound of it in the out-of-doors will leave whatever they are doing and answer the call. But close at hand? Ah, there is no word for it. The very universe is shattered, and you are too.

Jamie got secondhand confirmation of this the next evening. He went to the pub in search of Duncan, a search that turned out to be in vain, but he did settle into a conversation with old Tam, whose tongue had been well lubricated by this stage of the evening. When Jamie ventured a question about Duncan and the pipes, Tam fixed him with his eye, leaned across the table to Jamie, and whispered in something close to music, "When Duncan MacDuff plays the pipes, laddie, a change comes over all things on Erinsay. You can sense rumblings underground, as though spirits long stilled were being wakened. You can feel spirits moving in the air, gathering around the standing stones and the stone circles and the *sitheans*, the green mounds. Cattle in their stalls stir uneasily while Duncan plays, and it's my belief they are conscious of mysterious presences the rest of us cannot detect. As the sound of the pipes fills one valley and spills over into the next, you can feel, aye you can almost see, the hills readjusting to the contours of an earlier time, so that departed spirits who return at the call of the pipes will see their land just as it was long ago. If it's Friday, and you listen carefully once the music has stopped," and here Tam's voice dropped so low as to be barely distinguishable, "you can make out soft voices, brooding with one another in ways of speech long since extinguished on our island, just beyond sight but not quite beyond hearing."

Duncan had as long a family lineage as anyone on the island. His farm, a bit away from the main road going south from town and on the approach from the south to the Rutted Road, was a large one, and had been passed on from father to son for many generations. But Duncan, to his great sorrow, had had no sons, and although there were three stout sons-in-law who worked with him and would carry on the farm after him, it grieved him that there would be no male MacDuff on the land when he was gone.

A capacity for hard work was Duncan's character, and long with it a capacity for hard drinking, which was also his character. But as a drinker he never got mean. Whimsical, yes, and not above a trick or two at the pub, but he was not the kind of drinker who gets progressively uglier and uglier as closing time approaches, and then starts smashing at the host for refusing him a final dram after the clock has struck. Late in the evenings in the pub, when in his cups, was when Duncan played the pipes most gloriously. Early in the evenings in the pub he was a freeloader without equal, but all agreed that he paid full price once the pipes were out and working.

Then there was also the matter of the second sight.

On one of his afternoon walks, Jamie stopped at a small croft up the valley from the south road, to ask the way to what folk called the Faery Glen. The woman of the household, Jane Darley, invited him in "for a wee cup o' tea," and, having ascertained his name, introduced him in a loud voice to an old woman, obviously her mother, who was sitting in a chair before the fireplace. Although it was dark within the house, Jamie guessed, from the way she groped for his hand, that she was not only hard of hearing but of sight as well.

Over tea, the old woman, after asking two or three questions, lapsed into silence, and Jamie and the daughter carried on a desultory conversation. But as he rose to leave, the matriarch asked Jamie to come over beside her, and taking his hand in hers, muttered some words in a strange tongue. Jamie, not knowing what to make of it all, stammered a word of thanks and departure, but once outside the door asked Jane Darley if she had understood what the old woman said.

"Ah," came the response, "it was the Gaelic she was speaking, and I understand the words but not their meaning. She has the second sight," Jane Darley added, as matter-of-factly as though saying "She has a cold," "so it may be that she was telling you the story of what your life will be."

Jamie, whose belief in the second sight, the gift of seeing the future, was on a par with his belief in the objective reality of the Wee Folk, could nevertheless not thrust possible information about his own future into the pigeonhole of absolute skepticism. It was a subject about which even ordinary sight had proved singularly unhelpful.

"And could you be telling me, ma'am, her prediction about what the rest of my life will be? It's a subject in which I have a certain interest," he added, deferentially but not dispassionately.

"I can tell you the words," she repeated, "but not the meaning. Perhaps it will make sense to you, even if not to me. In the English it would be . . ." she paused a moment, and then continued, making a music of it,

> Two loves You'll have
> With names alike
> In different parts of time.

"Or something of the sort," she apologized, suddenly covered with embarrassment that she was presuming to instruct one who was obviously "an educated gentleman." "Do you understand what it means?"

"No," the educated gentleman responded truthfully, "it has no meaning to me, unless somewhere on Erinsay there is a woman named Annie . . . for it was an Annie that I loved back in Glasgow."

This was the fullest revelation Jamie had given to anyone of his mainland past, and Jane Darley registered the information without the movement of a facial muscle, though behind her passive exterior a furious mental exercise was going on as she processed this new data, filed it away carefully, and searched her mind for the one with whom it would be most exciting to share it.

Confronted by her ongoing silence, Jamie pressed his case. "*Is* there anyone on Erinsay with the name of Annie?"

It took only moments for the woman to sift through the entire female population of the island and reply, "We have only one of that name on Erinsay, and she has been married forty years. So at least," she said, smiling, as she turned to go back into the house, "you'll not be falling in love during your holiday."

Even more mystified, Jamie once again sought refuge in *Erinsay: Past and Present*, by W. E. G. Sheppherd, B. A., B.D., M.A. (with honors), and was presented with a mass of objective data about history, geography, geology, architecture, and artifacts. But more to the point for Jamie, the gentleman who had done such meticulous research over a lifetime had felt constrained to add an epilogue on a more personal note:

"Is there a magic in the isle? It's a mainlander's question, one never asked by us who live here. To us, what is, is. Someone's mother has the second sight? Very well, that is true about her if not about some others. The sound of faery music is heard over the sitheans of a Friday afternoon or eve? Even that is not surprising, the sitheans being what we know them to be—the abode of the Wee Folk. And if mainlanders scoff at such talk, so much the worse for those who have no sitheans by which to sit and listen.

"What the mainlanders might call magic, since it does not happen to them, is no more than our strict accounting of what does happen to us. When it happens, we report it to one another, and it enters our lore. And if, in recent times, we've not been so eager to report it to the mainland folk, that is simply because they cast a skeptical eye upon it and accuse us of tall tales. Their loss, we say.

"But there's a more important kind of magic in the isles, which has nothing to do with things supernatural. It's no more and no less than the peace of the place, woven about us like a web.

"To be sure, it's a hard life on Erinsay, scratching a living out of the peaty soil, and keeping the cattle in feed, and the fences mended, and bracing ourselves against storms that settle in for days on end, and one need not romanticize a life that has its full share of sorrow and disappointment. But if sorrow and disappointment are the common human lot, we consider ourselves lucky to live out our years on Erinsay. Some of our youth want no more of island living, and that's a choice we must grant them. But for most of us, the place we now are is the place we would ever choose to be.

"Who would want the city with its foul breath, when here you can see full across the inland loch and count the cormorants nesting on the farther cliffs, so clear is the air?

"Who would choose to visit friends, or go to work, by underground or tram, when here you can walk to your friends on winding roads caressed by human feet, and your work is just outside your door?

"Who would prefer an April morn in a crowded city park, when here you can watch the birthing of a lamb in spring, and see the new ones try their legs the first day out of the byre, glorious spots of white upon the still-green heather hillsides, frisking and jumping and stumbling, and following the ewes to drink and run and drink and run and drink again?

"What lad would choose to grub around the city streets peering in trash cans, when here he could be exploring pools at low tide, touching the belly of a starfish to see it curl up, or gathering mussels from the wet rocks and building a fire and boiling them in the very seawater itself?

"And then, for the rest of us, there comes the time each day when chores are done, and they've left us weary, but we are sitting on the front stoop of our farmhouses and know there's still a full two hours in the long summer eve before the darkness comes. And we watch, and every moment as the sun moves, there are new patterns of shadows on the rounding of the hills we have known since childhood, so that the same hills are always different, and still the same. There's strength in them, and strength as well in folk who live in their folds and are nursed for a lifetime by their bounty and their folds and are nursed for a lifetime by their bounty and their beauty, stern and simple though such gifts may be.

"And while we sit there it may be we'll hear a piper's music, mournful and sweet in the distance and blessing the twilight, or two sheep exchanging a mating call, or the larks singing, wild and ecstatic, a song above their nest, or down past the beach, out on the skerries, the plaintive barking of the seals.

"Those things are a magic, too, and a kind of peace.

"We believe our loved ones in their graves are also at peace, embraced by the sod, warmed by the sun, watered by the heavens, and nourished by the whole lifetime of their memories. For part of what it means to live on the isle is to know that we will die on the isle, and for all of us who live here the story of death is part of the story of life. We do not hide from it as they do on the mainland. The bodies stay with us, three days in the house, and then, until the last trump, are nestled in the ground. Sad it is when a loved one dies, but then they're only as far from us as the graveyard.

"So when we live, we live with the land; and when we die, the land lives in us. And that, too, is a kind of peace."

When Duncan MacDuff appeared in the pub that Wednesday evening, there was a general move to clear away some space, for he had brought his pipes, and, with the proper sort of coaxing, he could be expected to warm them up before the evening was over. But there was a delicate timing to it, a ritual in which each one knew his part.

"Will you not give us a tune, Duncan?" would be the first query, destined, as all knew, to be turned down flat. And why not? The evening was young, and he was not yet, as he would say (with just the slightest hint of indelicacy) "in the mood." "And besides," he would continue when pressed, "I haven't touched the pipes for many a day, and the evening air is far too dry to do them justice."

The proper response to this carefully modulated delineation was to offer Duncan, as counterpoise to the dryness of the evening, one whiskey neat, which, when offered, would be graciously accepted and gratefully consumed. The empty glass would be replaced by a full one that would go the way of its predecessor. The process quickly made Duncan more expansive.

"Ah, Donald!" he said on this occasion, spying a young shepherd from Mulgarry, the town on the Other Side of the island, "sure, it's good to be seeing you on This Side of the island for once. I hear it's the McCallum lass you're courting, so you no longer have time for the rest of us, is that the way of it?"

Donald, covered with mortification at both the directness and the correctness of Duncan's sally, instantly lost the power of speech, a phenomenon he also experienced in the presence of the object of his courtship, and Duncan, sensing that he had overplayed his hand against a newcomer to the game, withdrew the barb by responding, "And sure, Donald, if there be occasion for a wedding in the future, I might just bring the pipes along and have a go for you and the lassie, if it were pleasing to the both of you."

The offer was generous. It was also redundant. Everyone in the room, Duncan included, knew with certainty that whether the offer was accepted or not, the pipes would be brought to the wedding party after the service, and that Duncan would play not only until the bride and groom had left, and not only until the last bottle had been opened, but until the last bottle had been consumed and it was absolutely clear that no more bottles would be forthcoming.

The gathered assembly was unwilling, however, to wait until Donald Kibbie's slow-moving courtship had been brought to its expected consummation.

"How about a warm-up right now?" was the next question, to which a doleful declination was offered. "This isn't the night, lads. My lips are sore and cracked, and I'm thinking I'd better rest them." Decoded, this observation led to the placing on Duncan's table of another malt whiskey, undiluted by such pollutants as water.

The ritual continued. Each request for music would be met by a polite and gentle refusal, each refusal would be met by a polite and gentle act of replenishment, as from an invisible hand, of another dram. Each dram would have the effect of weakening, ever so slightly, the initial and seemingly definitive refusal to play. The issue at stake, if one were a gambling man, was never whether or not Duncan would play, but only when and after how many.

Finally, five or six drinks down the line (which was about par for the course on an average evening), the threshold of resistance would be overcome.

"Well, lads," came the long-awaited response, "its's been a long time since I blew the pipes, and it's murdering the music I'll be doing, but since I have them here, perhaps you'll excuse me if I just try a tune or two. It'll serve as practice," he added, turning again to the luckless Donald, "for your wedding, if," he concluded with a stern look, "you ever get up nerve enough to ask the lass straight out."

And then there was another ritual, for which one not an expert in the pipes could never provide satisfactory rubrics. Fetching a large collection of apparently miscellaneous objects, Duncan fitted them together with a care that could only have been motivated by love, and then, after placing the whole contraption over his shoulder, he filled the great bag with air, and with a squeeze of his elbow persuaded the instrument to exhale an initial moan that soon mounted into a battle cry capable of summoning both the quick and the dead. As he curved his fingers delicately over the chanter, the artist in the man took over, and after what seemed at first no more than a series of finger-exercises but gradually turned into "The Battle for the Bridge of Perth," Duncan MacDuff was off and away.

He could surely have played the night out (as, according to both legend and living memory, he had done many times before), had it not been a Wednesday, rather than a Saturday, and tasks to do in the morning. Thursday was not the biblically appointed day of rest.

Jamie fell into step with Duncan as the crowd dispersed, for they would be covering the same ground on the first part of their respective journeys. Duncan, aroused by the piping and mellowed by the malt, lapsed into a philosophical mood, once he saw that this Outsider was hanging on to his every word.

"It's a funny thing about the pipes," he mused, as they walked in the darkness, "they've seen us through victories and defeats, and they've been solace when we've not been lucky in love and means for joy when we have been.

"They're our heritage, Mr. Stuart, part of what makes us who we are. You'll find other nations sharing the fife and the drum, or playing trumpets in their saloons and in their beer halls, and you can hear an organ or a violin anywhere, and never know what country you're in. But you will never, never," and his voice rose, "you'll never hear the pipes but what you'll know it's a Scot you'll be hearing, and it's bonny Scotland and you'll be thinking of and remembering and celebrating, wherever in the world you are. And if it's not the case," he concluded, "you can be sure you're confronting some filthy imposter trying to pass himself off as one of us."

Having delivered this weighty observation, Duncan turned to the side of the road, unbuttoned his fly, and relieved himself.

"So it's a mighty power the pipes possess," he resumed, as if there had been no pause. "There's nowhere in the world a Scot can hear the pipes without he stands tall and proud. You can summon a Scot out of a mammoth crowd in any part of the world, if you simply do a turn on the pipes. And sure, you can summon the dead as well, if you know the ways to go about it. But of that," he suddenly concluded, "I'd best not be talking," especially in the presence of a stranger, Jamie surmised.

Duncan, as if convinced that he had trespassed across some well-marked conversational boundary, lapsed into an uncharacteristic silence that Jamie was unwilling to accept as definitive. Summon the dead? Was this part of the set of tales Hamish had been saying were at the center of Duncan's world?

"Summon the dead, Mr. MacDuff?" he prompted. "And would you be telling me how that's done?"

"Nay, that I wouldn't," was the grumpy response. "There's some things," he concluded, "best left unsaid."

Now it so happened that Jamie had in his jacket a small flask that he carried on his island outings, as protection against the cold. Solicitously anticipating the possibility of a chill in Duncan MacDuff's person, Jamie offered to share the contents of the flask as a remedy against the effects of a cool evening breeze on the nervous system. It was not the first time such preventive medicine had been practiced on Erinsay.

"And how do you summon the dead, Mr. MacDuff?" Jamie asked deferentially a few moments later, hoping that he had allowed time for the elixir to do its work.

It was soon clear that he had.

"It's a gift passed on from father to son," Duncan said confidentially, "A certain way of playing, so that when it's heard in the nether realms, the dead, even if cold in their graves . . ."

His voice trailed off. "Cold they are, aye, cold they are, like even those still alive can be cold of a summer evening."

Duncan found himself silenced by the degree of coldness apportioned to those yet living. Jamie was quick to offer further medicinal fortification.

"Sure, and it's a funny thing," Duncan warmed and fortified, continued in a moment, "but my father, and his father before him, had learned a trick of playing the pipes that he passed on to me (though it will die with me, since I have no son to whom to pass it on), so that if you play the pipes in a certain way of a Friday, you can summon the spirits from the past. And they come and join the Wee Folk around the green mounds, for, as you know, the Wee Folk gather there, and woe to any man who is standing on the green mounds of a Friday when the Wee Folk are there and the souls of the departed are there too, aroused by the power of the pipes. . . . Spirit them off to the past they will, and that's a fact."

Duncan, apparently envisioning such a confrontation, lapsed once more into meditative silence, during which he shivered perceptibly. "Cold as a tomb, the night, isn't it, lad?" he queried, not changing the subject.

"Would another nip warm you," Jamie responded. It was not a question.

"Since you're so kind," Duncan responded, reaching out his hand automatically for the now near-empty flask, without breaking step.

"But surely," Jamie pressed his advantage a moment later, "all of that was long ago. The Wee Folk have not appeared for many years, as I've heard tell."

Duncan's demeanor changed. Indignation replaced meditation. "Och, lad, to whom have you been listening to hear such driveling talk as that?" he asked. "The parson, maybe, or Aimee Truesdell, who's no proper Scot herself? It may be," he continued, leaning toward Jamie and taking him by the arm, either to speak in greater confidence or simply to steady himself, "it may be that the Wee Folk are not so powerful as they once were, and so can no longer by themselves drag folk out of here and now, and into the faery realm, leastwise I've not heard so much of it in recent times. But believe me, lad, when it's summoning the Wee Folk you are, by stamping on the faery mounds and shouting 'Friday!' at the same time the dead are being brought back by the sound of the pipes, then you'd better believe—you'd better believe—the Wee Folk and the dead together can overpower any mortal and take the poor creature back to who knows what and where. And that's God's own truth," he concluded, placing a theological capstone on the argument.

They were standing at the point where their ways parted. Assessing Duncan's ability to make it home as of a high order of probability, and remembering that Duncan had had years of practice at the endeavor, Jamie bade him goodnight and turned toward the manse, with Duncan's parting shot in his ear:

"So remember, lad, if you want to stay out of trouble, stay off the faery mounds of a Friday, and never, never say the word 'Friday!' when you are near them, especially," he paused and repeated for emphasis as he started on down the road, "especially if you hear at the same time the sound of the pipes of Duncan MacDuff."

While Jamie did not relate the full conversation with Duncan to Hamish, he did share enough of it to raise the complicated question of whether there might be simultaneous activity on the part of the Wee Folk and the departed spirits sufficient to summon into the past those who dared invade the green mounds when Duncan's pipes were playing.

It was a complicated problem, and Hamish was not about to be drawn into such speculation, not because it was so complicated but because it was so heterodox. The very suggestion demanded a coming together of Christian faith and pagan lore that his divinity school training still made repugnant.

"But it reminds me," he remarked, in his sole concession to the query, "of an old Celtic prophecy. . . . Let me see, how does it go?"

A prolonged silence on Hamish's part, supportively shared by Jamie, yielded no answer, not even when stimulated by the liturgical experience of the lighting of Hamish's pipe at both the beginning and the ending of the interval.

Hamish finally heaved his not inconsiderable frame out of

the easy chair and rummaged in the upper shelf of the bookcase. After he had removed several volumes, blown off the
dust, examined and then deposited them on the desk in dis-
orderly array, a triumphant gasp escaped him.

"Ah! Just as I thought. Here it is, though its origins are on
Rhum or Canna rather than Erinsay. Let's see . . . ," and he
muttered over the Gaelic lines several times before coming up
with translation:

> When the pipes are blown
> and the ground is shaken
> Then time's reversed.

"Sure it is, old Duncan must have been thinking about that
saying, and thrust himself into the very middle of it.

"I don't really know what it means," Hamish mused, "unless
maybe some Christian influences have been at work on it." He
warmed to this gratifying possibility. " 'The pipes,' . . . let's see,
the pipes could be the trumpet sound of the last judgment, and
the 'shaken ground' could be the dead rising out of their graves,
for there's a lot of that in early Christian art. . . ." But he continued, almost to himself and slightly crestfallen, "No, that
won't quite work, for in Christian thought it's not that time is
'reversed' but simply that it ceases to be. I wonder about a Platonic influence . . ."

Here was a rich vein for speculation, and Hamish was off in
a private reverie, in which contemplation of eternity blocked
off, for the moment at least, the world of time.

Jamie, having a more prosaic mind not much influenced by
Christian considerations, let alone Platonic influences, but
still full of the power of Duncan's own description, decided
that "shaking ground" could well refer to ground stamped
upon (even though the verse made no reference to shouting

"Friday"), and that old Duncan, his imagination well lubricated by malt whiskey, had simply insinuated himself into a Celtic prophecy, assuming that his own "pipes" were being described, and that "the reversal" of time meant summoning the dead back to life.

Thus reassured that Duncan's fanciful conclusions could be safely dismissed as unwarranted extrapolation from a fanciful Celtic rune, Jamie turned back to the more substantial and more immediately satisfying challenge of doing justice to the pile of buttered scones, topped with marmalade, that Jennie had just brought in for their afternoon tea.

Friday week Hamish was planning to walk to the Hendersons', well down toward the south end of the island, to work out details for the baptism, come Sabbath, of the newest Henderson, a daughter at whose birth Jennie had been midwife only a few weeks before. Since the Hendersons had produced a new Henderson on the average of one every fourteen months over the last eight years, and Hamish had baptized them all in the kirk in identical services, he had suggested to Maggie Henderson that the trip was unnecessary; all the participants in the service, save the newest arrival, were by now routinely familiar with their parts and scarcely required another dress rehearsal. But Mrs. Henderson had been insistent. "This might be Granny's last baptism," she had replied, using a phrase invoked on the occasion of each of the last five baptisms, and for her sake they wanted, as the island phrase had it, "to do it right."

So Hamish and Jennie were invited for a high tea, with a three o'clock departure scheduled. They were going to make an outing of it.

At five minutes to three, just as Jennie had laced her walking shoes, young Davie Grace appeared at the door of the manse, all in a sweat, having run down from the north end of the island, under stern parental admonition. The baby had colic, he panted, his mother had no medicine, and they were frightened. Would Mrs. Bell have a look in?

It was not a request to be declined. Hamish would simply have to explain Jennie's absence to the Hendersons. But with all the preparations Mrs. Henderson would have made for a high tea . . .

Jennie had no answer. "Just pop up to Jamie's room and see if he won't walk with you and take my place," she proposed. "I saw him go upstairs just moments ago." And she was off to the Graces' with Davie, three miles to the north.

Jamie, apprised of the situation, was compliant. He was getting a bit tired of hiking alone, and Hamish could point out items of interest along the south road during the hour's walk that he might previously have missed.

They started out only about ten minutes behind schedule, Jamie realizing immediately that he would have to trim his brisk walking gait (he was getting in better shape each day) to accommodate his older and stouter companion. They passed the hotel and the kirk and were soon in the fold of the low hills that had to be crossed on the way to the Hendersons'.

As they negotiated a sharp bend in the road with some ruins nearby—an old byre and farm cottage by the look of them—Hamish, who had been commenting on the gradual but perceptible shift in island occupations from fishing to sheepherding and farming, suddenly noticed where they were and said, "Ah, look Jamie! There is one of the sitheans, the green mounds we were talking about the other evening, where the legends say the Wee Folk used to grab off the brash ones who trespassed and stamped on their land. . . . A good thing we're not a hundred years earlier, or they might be after us for coming even this close."

He was still chuckling at this mild witticism when both of them heard sounds—not sounds of faery music or melodies from a nether realm, but good, earthy, honest Scottish sounds. For somewhere across the hills, Duncan MacDuff was tuning up his pipes, no doubt having left the Friday afternoon chores to his sons-in-law, the better to practice his pipes for the ceilidh scheduled for Saturday only a fortnight off. Or maybe, thought Hamish, he means to play the pipes at the Henderson baptism, a thought that left him caught in a tension between personal delight and liturgical chagrin.

In a moment the tuning was over and Duncan was in full command of a strathspey. An impulse seized Jamie.

"Keep on going, Hamish," he said, already turning his back on his walking companion. "I'll catch up to you in a moment." For Jamie had decided to try an experiment. The prerequisites were clear. It must include (1) a bagpiper endowed with Duncan's unique skills, (2) a nearby sithean, (3) full of Wee Folk who resented the invasion of their space, and (4) someone able to orchestrate the ongoing chorus of "Friday! Friday! Friday!"

The notion had come to him full-blown when he realized that he could emulate the conditions Duncan had specified. Jamie had access to a piper, a sithean, and his own voice to keep the chorus of "Friday" alive and well. Maybe (here Jamie was succumbing to their spell) involvement in such activities might entice the Wee Folk into action.

Worth a try anyhow.

Walking to the center of the sithean, Jamie began to stamp his foot upon the sod in rhythm with the pipes, shouting "Friday! Friday! Friday!"

The Island Then
Moragh McPherson

 was standing on a green mound.

How I got there, what I was doing before I got there, my name, my background, my wife (if I have a wife), my job—all that was blank. For just a moment there was a feel of music, and of powerful forces pulling and tugging, but even as I sought to recall them, they were lost beyond retrieval.

It was as though I had just that moment woken from a dream, save that with this waking there slipped away not only the memory of the dream but also the identity of the dreamer.

So if I say, as I must, that my earliest memory is of standing on a green mound, I speak the simple truth.

Somewhere within that primal moment, I noticed that there was a barn nearby, beyond which was a farmyard, and that beyond them both was a cottage. I saw two boys, ten and twelve perhaps, trying not very successfully to drive a recalcitrant cow from the far pasture toward the barnyard. Their action offered a possible orientation to time of day: perhaps it was the hour for milking.

I was about to hail the lads when I realized that there was nothing I could ask them without appearing an utter fool. Who lives here? Where is the village? Where in the world am I? Who are you? And, what was I to reply to their inevitable query, "And who are you?"

I decided I was not yet ready for human encounter. I would explore the countryside instead, hoping some familiar object would trigger my temporarily ailing memory.

So I stepped down from the mound and onto the road, deep-grooved from wagon tracks, and peaceably meandering around the edge of a small gorse-covered hill. I arbitrarily turned right instead of left. The terrain seemed vaguely familiar, as though I had been transported into a land of earlier dreams, but a land in which I could not find my way or even get my bearings. I walked through a quiet landscape, and finally saw a short man walking in my direction. He spied me also; encounter was inevitable.

"Good day." His greeting was cordially delivered, though accompanied by an ill-concealed glance of curiosity at my clothes.

"A good day it is," I responded, giving back no more information than I had received, since indeed I had none to offer. And then, curiosity and confusion overcoming caution, I continued, "Begging your pardon, sir, but I'm a stranger in these parts . . ."

"Aye," he broke in, giving me now the careful and straightforward scrutiny that was legitimized by my self-revelation. Having completed his examination of me, he gazed at the sky, then at the earth, cleared his throat, winked, and replied, "Sure it is you don't look to be from these parts."

I had to ask him a question to forestall his asking me any questions. "Could you be telling me," I improvised, pointing to the rear, "whose is the farm I passed just a moment ago?"

He considered this question for a substantial time, during which he once again gazed at the sky, then at the earth, cleared his throat, and winked, before replying, "Aye, that be the Widow McPherson's."

Assuming this would be the extent of his response, and not feeling particularly enlightened by it, I stared blankly at him, at a loss. Something in my passive silence must have emboldened him, for he unleashed a torrent of information.

"I hear she be lookin' quite desperate for someone to help with the planting, her husband bein' dead these three years afore, and her hired hand having up and left for the mainland just like that"—he made a gesture indicating flight, before picking up in midstream—"what with the spring plowin' still waitin' to be done. And she with the two boys, who'll not be up to keepin' the old ox on a straight furrow for many a season."

Apparently exhausted by this outburst, the old man gazed again at the sky, then at the earth, cleared his throat and winked, a ritual that could terminate as well as initiate a conversation.

"Well, I thank you kindly, sir," I responded, "and a good day to you." My mind was already turning over the possible import of this information.

The old man continued his walk, soon passing out of sight, while I sat down by the side of the road to consider both the plight of the Widow McPherson and the plight of . . . whoever I was.

Certain practicalities, calling for action, were emerging. I was fiercely hungry, it would soon be nightfall, and I had nowhere to stay. While I had no recollection of having done farm work (or any other kind of work) before, I assumed that I could learn under instruction, so that at least I could earn my keep until my memory stopped playing tricks on me and I could rediscover who and where I was, and whatever I was supposed to be about.

So I retraced my steps, and when I got back to the green mound I turned off the road, walked around the barn, and crossed the barnyard. There was no sign of the lads, who by now must have gotten the cow inside and were probably milking and doing chores, so I went to the door of the cottage and knocked. A tall woman, with a tired face that might once have been beautiful, opened the door.

Seeing a strange man, she withdrew slightly.

"Aye?" she said warily.

"Be you Mrs. McPherson?" I asked deferentially.

"Aye," she responded with scarcely a change of tone or posture.

"Please, ma'am," I responded, "I mean you no harm. But I understand from your neighbor that you have need of a hand to help with the plowing, and I hoped you might consider me."

"It's true, we've not got enough help just now, until the bairns are stouter," she said, relaxing a bit, but still wary. "But I don't believe," she ventured, searching her memory, "I've seen you before. Have you worked other farms on the island?"

My reply was an evasion. "Well, to be honest, ma'am you

may have to show me how to do one or two things, but I'm fair willing to be taught by the lads or by you, if that's your pleasure."

She was not reassured by my transparent admission of inexperience. "I couldn't pay you till after the harvest time," she responded, as though to discourage me, and I thought she was moving to close to door. But then, apparently deciding midstream that any help would be better than none, she continued, ". . . except for meals, of course, and a place to sleep." She hurried on, already having reached a decision. "There's a place in the cow barn with a cot, and there's a shelf too," she continued, "though from the looks of you," she added, noting that I had no luggage, "you'll not need much space to store your belongings. And it has a door to keep the stray animals out, and it's fair close to the water trough. The lads and I sleep in the house," she concluded firmly, leaving no doubt about the ground rules for hired hands.

"Mrs. McPherson, you're very kind," I responded, once more trying to reassure her, "and if you find I cannot do the work, you have only to say the word and I'll be on my way." For I was sure that I would soon have my memory back and be able to leave of my own accord.

"Fair enough," she responded, "but I hope the work agrees with you, for you look sturdy enough, and we've great need of some strong shoulders. The men on the nearby farms come when they can," she explained, relaxing a bit, "but they've their own crops to plant and harvest, and I don't feel free to ask them, if you understand my meaning. So it's glad I am if you can help us. Angus and Tammas are in the barn and can show you the place for sleeping. And now, I'll just get back to preparing the evening meal, if you'll excuse me. We'll eat shortly, Mr. . . . Mr. . . . , what were you saying your name was?"

Caught off guard, I said the first name that came to mind. I don't know why.

"Jamie," I said, "you can call me Jamie."

Mrs. McPherson was already seated at the kitchen end of the table when I entered the cottage, having found my cot in the byre and washed at the trough. There were three other chairs, including one opposite her. I chose not to sit there, assuming it to be the place her husband had once occupied, and sat instead on the far side of the table across from Tammas. And that was most appropriate, I discovered, for the elder lad, Angus Jr., took the seat once occupied by his father, that being the family custom I discovered, and it was wonderful how gravely he took over being head of the household.

Once we were seated, Mrs. McPherson, looking him full in the face, said, "Angus?"—not so much a question as a cue— and he, responding, bowed his head as a sign to us to do the same, and said, very softly, "For what we now receive, good Lord, give us grateful hearts, and be with Daddy and wee Fione." Tammas and Mrs. McPherson said "Amen," and I, caught off guard, and not yet understanding the last part of the prayer, was silent. But at later meals (for the ritual was always repeated) I, too, said "Amen."

We had potatoes and sprouts and small bits of a kind of meat (rabbit, I think it was), along with strong tea, and a pudding for desert. We did not talk too much that first evening, the lads being shy in the presence of a stranger, but we did discuss the plowing and the planting that would begin on the morrow, bright and early.

When the meal was completed, Mrs. McPherson rose and said to me, "Jamie, the lads and I will be going for a short walk to see old Mrs. Andrews at the next farm, for she's been ailing for some time. We'll be back before sundown for an evening cup of tea. So tonight you're welcome to sit here while we're gone, if you wish." She was making two things clear: first, that the walk did not include me, and second, that sitting in the cottage of an evening was not a privilege ordinarily extended to a hired hand. It was a way she had, of stating certain things in an indirect way, as I gradually came to know.

I thanked her and remained, sharing the room with the cat who had been rubbing our legs throughout the meal, hoping for a morsel.

The furnishings of the cottage were sparse. The living area was already getting dark, since the only light came from tiny windows carved out of the thick walls. It had one further chair, with a small table beside it, on which lay the only book in the room, a huge family Bible, next to an oil lamp. The dining table, from which we had just arisen, was rectangular, with a chair on each side. The tiny kitchen was just beyond. A small fireplace was fueled with peat brought in from a pile outside that someone had stacked against the house. The two lads, I gathered, shared a room, next to the other room in which, presumably, Mrs. McPherson slept.

I did not prowl around, that hardly seeming a right thing to do, but I did, after sitting a few moments, open the Bible, and in the fading light, examined a hand-written genealogy, inscribed on the first pages in spaces provided for it. The newest entries were, "Angus, Jr., born August 11, 1813," "Tammas, born September 3, 1815," and "Fione, born February 23, 1826, died February 23, 1826." Above their names were inscribed the names "Moragh Duffie McPherson, born February 17, 1796," and "Angus McPherson, born July 18, 1791," and uniting their names, "married June 20, 1812."

After Angus' birthday had been added, in a different color of ink, "died February ?, 1826."

I wondered at the question mark. Later I learned that Angus Sr. had gone on a fishing voyage with a friend, that they had been caught in a winter gale that started on February 18, and that the two bodies had not been washed ashore until February 22, the day after the storm abated. So the exact date of his death was unknown. Indeed, a number of dates turned out to be only approximations.

With a bit of figuring, I concluded that it was now the year 1829, since the old man on the road had told me that the Widow McPherson's husband had been dead three years. I now knew that the Widow McPherson's Christian name was Moragh. I knew the ages of Angus Jr. and Tammas to be thirteen and eleven respectively, or just about, since their birthdays were in August and September and it seemed to be mid summer. And I knew that long after the two of them there had been a daughter, Fione, stillborn it would appear from the entry. Fione was prematurely delivered, I later learned, the day after Mrs. McPherson got the news of her husband's death. So there had been a double funeral in the kirk, and Mrs. McPherson became all at the same time both the Widow McPherson and a woman grieving the loss of a daughter as well as a husband.

And that was the sum of my wisdom.

No, not quite. For I knew one other thing, though not from the family Bible. I knew that I, a total stranger, had been taken in, and that the three of them, not knowing who I was (no more did I), were trusting of me. And that, along with a full stomach and assurance of a place to sleep, was a cause of contentment.

When they returned, we had our cup of tea, and then, not

too long after nine-thirty, Mrs. McPherson, in her indirect but forceful way, took charge again. First she put down her cup of tea, and then she put her hands together in her lap and straightened her back. "And now, Jamie," she said, rising from her seat, "you'll be wanting to get some sleep before morning, I expect, with all the plowing to do, and we've not got a mind to leave you more tired than is necessary." Having delivered these instructions, her face relaxed into something almost like a smile. She looked not so old and tired as before when she said, "And it's glad we are that you've come to help us."

And I, taking my cue, bade her and the lads good night, and made my way to the byre, where I found she had already made up the cot for me and even left a pitcher of water beside it.

I lay down. A moment later Angus Jr. was rapping on the door and telling me that the porridge was piping hot.

When I first heard the rapping, I had no idea where I was. I would probably have gone back into a deep sleep, had I not also heard, very faintly at first, another sound. Someone was singing, and the song was faint since, as I discovered upon getting out of bed, it was coming from inside the cottage. It was not the singing of a boy, so the not unreasonable inference of my still drowsy brain was that it must be the voice of Mrs. McPherson.

I strained to hear. The music seemed distantly familiar. Somewhere, surely . . . but the memory, if it was a memory, eluded me.

The words eluded me too for they were in another tongue. Gaelic, no doubt.

Vair me o, o ro van o, came the sounds from the house, the first part of a chorus apparently, for it was frequently repeated.

Vair me o, o ro van ee,

Vair me o, o ru o ho, the music soaring upward with the words *ru o ho,* and then, in English, as I could now make out:

Sad am I without thee.

I must have known it before, somewhere, for the line of the melody I could almost anticipate; either that, or it released wellsprings of emotion deep in the human heart, putting into music what all our hearts feel and cannot easily express until another does it for us, after which we say, "Of course!"

However that may be, the verses began with an almost jaunty line of melody that became wistful and forlorn at the end, befitting the English words with which each rendering of the chorus concluded.

Did it speak of a part of my own forgotten past, so as to draw a response from within me of which I was not even consciously aware? Or was I simply moved by the unaffected voice of the singer, whom I had met scarce twelve hours earlier, and for whom the words seemed heavy with meaning?

For moved I was. But I did not have time to find out why, for when I went outside the byre, the better to listen (but covering my curiosity by going to the trough to douse my head), the singing stopped abruptly, which I took as a sign that my presence had been noted through the tiny kitchen window.

Inside the house a few moments later, I asked, "And what was the music you were singing just now, Mrs. McPherson? Fair bonny it was."

But she, covered with embarrassment, and blushing even through a well-tanned face, could only murmur, "Oh tosh, Jamie, 'tis only a song from Eriskay, 'The Love Lilt' I think they call it. I hardly even know it." After which she retreated to the range and busied herself stirring the porridge furiously.

And I sat in silence at the table, fearing I had spoken out of turn, for it was not just embarrassment that sent her to the stove, but pain in her voice and sadness in her face.

The pain and sadness were for her husband, and although outwardly she always appeared strong and firm, as I came to know her it was clear that even after three years, her inner wound had not healed and her loneliness was intense. Angus was present to her far beyond any direct telling of it, for every so often she would say to her sons things like, "Ah, but your father would be proud of you." Or "You like the jam, Angus? It was your father's favorite too." Or "Your father made that stool, Tammas; see how well it's put together."

Even with me it would come out. Explaining the fencing, she would add, "Angus hoped to build a gate there," or, when the house seemed crowded on a rainy day, "Angus planned to add another room, once we were a bit ahead."

And now and then, when she was alone or thought she could not be overhead, it was the Eriskay "Love Lilt" she would sing, the music I had heard that first morning, and it was to her dead husband she was singing, beyond any doubting of it. What can I say of her voice, save that it was clear and pure, and that when she sang the chorus, and came to "*Vair me o, o ru o ho,*" she soared up to its high notes like a gull rising on a warm draft, with no outward motion, effortlessly, freely, cleanly. But the final line, "Sad am I without thee," was always low and troubled, just as the music itself went, and her voice would tremble when she sang it. And I could feel that the words of the second verse, "Dark the night and wild the sea," held a special terror for her, since that was how he had died—out in a wild sea in the darkness of the night—and in her imagination she had surely died with him a hundred times the death he had died but once.

So she sang to him her song of love and sadness, a love that was full of grief, both in the music and in the singing of the music. And yet, I could also feel that with some elemental faith she believed his spirit hovered near and heard her. And that was surely a solace and a further reason why she sang.

The sailors on the isles, as I later learned, believe that those who drown at sea return in spirit in the bodies of the gulls, to hover and brood above the fierce waters, safe now and at peace. It is not a likely tale as far as I can see, but for her sake I wished it so, for there never was a time on the croft that the gulls were not near at hand, flying inland the few hundred yards from the sea, soaring overhead and then swooping down for a piece of bread or a bit of feed the cattle had not consumed. Many is the time I saw her, while hanging up the clothes to dry, throw a bit of scone in the air for the gulls to swoop at and catch in their beaks before it hit the ground, her lithe form all alive with the gesture of throwing.

Was she communing with her dead husband when she did that? I would not have asked and she would not have said, at least to me, but it was a sight of loveliness to see her body all free and graceful in those moments, full of a fierce love both sad and beautiful.

In those first days when we were doing the plowing, the gulls, hundreds of them, would follow us and alight on each upturned furrow to see what morsels they could wrestle from the soil. Had I known at that time of the legend the sailors tell, I would have hoped that Angus was in that long white train of watchers of the land—his land—and that he was getting sustenance from the fruits of his earlier toil.

Ah, but she was loyal to his memory! A year after his death, as I later learned, she had been visited by the only "eligible" on the island, with a view (as he put it to his friends) to matrimony. But he had been too hasty a suitor, and she had dismissed him almost rudely, feeling that such interest in another man within a year of Angus's death would be not only unseemly but a betrayal of her love for Angus and their life together. One year later there was a wedding in the kirk, but it was not Moragh McPherson who was the young man's bride, but one Jeannie Bartholemew, and she from the far side of the island.

And now, a full three years after Angus's death, there was no one on the island of a proper age. And though she must at times have ached for a man, she never gave indication of it, but gave herself instead to the farm and to her lads, whom she was training to work the farm, and marry, and cultivate the land long after she was gone.

At first, taking my cue from that initial evening, I would dismiss myself after the evening meal, and go for a walk in the island twilight or work in the barn. When I was dog tired from a hard day in the fields or cutting the peat, I would go straight to the corner of the farm that held my cot and lie down. At such times I would try to remember the past and puzzle out who I was, seeking faint memories that might give me clues. But that was a futile exercise, as I discovered, and I did it less and less, not only because it gave no help, but also because I found the present absorbing enough so as not to worry overmuch about the past. Indeed, there were times when I almost feared the day when I would discover who I was and be forced to leave the croft and perhaps the island in order to resume my former life.

Angus and Tammas soon became my friends. Deliberate in manner and grave of countenance was Angus Jr., and I reasoned that he and his father had been very close, so much did the shadow of the death still hang over him. Tammas, by contrast, was a towhead with a face full of freckles and an impudent streak that sometimes tested the patience of his mother and older brother. After some initial condescension, while both of them were teaching me the ways of life on the croft and could exploit my ignorance, they accepted me as a working partner and a friend. Their mother, though always cautious and withdrawn when I was near her, was fair and kind in her treatment of me. But I still felt an intruder in those evenings when the three of them rested in the living room together after the day's work. For I knew, from now and then overhearing words they exchanged, that those were occasions when she shared her stories of their father, wanting the memory of him to stay fresh, so they would stand tall and proud as the sons of Angus McPherson.

But one night as I got up to take my leave, the meal being ended, she unexpectedly said, "You're welcome to sit with us, Jamie, if you have a mind to." It was an act of thoughtfulness, but even more it was an act of acceptance, and though I made excuses that one night, being flustered, if the truth be told, I stayed the next, and from then on it was our custom.

Sometimes we would talk about the island and its people. Once she taught the boys and me a song, though it was not *Vair me o*. Sometimes we would just sit, tired in body from a long day, deliciously absorbing the healing and refreshing rest.

But the end of the evening was always the same, a kind of ritual. A bit past nine she would say, as though the thought had never occurred to her before, but was all a fresh discovery, "I think I'll just have a cup of tea." And then, to the lads and myself, "Will you be joining me?" And we would say, "Aye," as though on cue, and there would be a cup apiece and sometimes a scone to go with it, and then, no later than about nine-thirty, she would put her hands in her lap, and straighten her back and say to us, "Well now, you'll be wanting your sleep, I expect." And rising from her chair she would give us our cue to rise from our chairs, and her saying "Good night" to us would give us our cue to say "Good night" to her.

And later, though not at first, she would say to Tammas though never to Angus who was older, "Give Jamie a hug for good night, *that's* the lad!" But never did she herself offer to give Jamie a hug for goodnight, and it was not my place to suggest it, though as more and more nights passed I would have wished it so.

Once, on toward the equinox, when the lads were out playing some game in the barnyard, she sat withdrawn for the longest time, and finally, breaking the silence with an effort, she said, "I hope you'll be forgiving me, Jamie, for my lack of speech. It's dull and heavy I feel this night, for this is the wedding anniversary of Angus and myself . . . and I still miss him so much." And at the words, "I miss him so much," all of the strength and power and stubborn pride of the woman gave way, and there she was, quietly weeping, dabbing at her eyes with her handkerchief, and saying, "Excuse me, Jamie, I'm sorry to be so foolish."

And I wanted to say that it was not foolish to grieve the loss of those we love, and that I understood and wanted to grieve with her, but I had no words for it. So, feeling pity and sorrow, and a sense that I was still a stranger who should not view her grief, I got up to leave, and as I went by on the way to the door I put a hand on her shoulder, ever so lightly, just to comfort her, and was already withdrawing it, feeling she would consider it forward, when I felt her hand on mine and heard her say, "Thank you, Jamie," and then, as swift as her hand had been placed there it was withdrawn, as though to tell me she knew it had strayed where it never belonged, and she was out of her chair and out of the room, offering a muffled "Goodnight," before I was full aware of what was happening.

But I was soon full aware, for my hand tingled half the night and my whole body as well.

I soon learned to do the chores that were too demanding for the lads. Now and then she would make a direct request to me, and after a while I even became bold enough to make suggestions. I would say something like, "Mrs. McPherson, wouldn't it be a good idea to put a stone path here?" or "Don't you think, Mrs. McPherson, that it would be a help to fence off this pasture for the cows so the sheep will not be cropping the grass?" And she would say "Yes, Jamie" or "No, Jamie," and I would do her bidding.

For a while this formal manner of our speaking did not bother me. I was the hired hand, and she was not, so it was fitting to our relationship that she was "Mrs. McPherson" and I was "Jamie." But I began to feel awkward about it, for she seemed more and more not just the employer, but a person with whom I liked to be, and one whose voice carried a kind of "music of my heart," just as the song said, the song that she sang about another. And even though there were times when the desire came upon me, and I would have wanted to take her in my arms, I knew that she would judge it forward of me, and a betrayal of her dead husband if she did other than rebuff me. So I would take long walks, or swim at a nearby beach, or

sometimes dream of her in ways it would not be proper to acknowledge to another.

For she was a fair and bonny woman. Old she had seemed
at that first meeting, but I no longer saw her so. Whatever
women I might have known before in that blocked-out life of
mine, I was sure there could have been none like her. She gave
of herself in kindness and gentleness, in little acts of love to
her sons, and considerations for me, that touched me at
depths I was sure had never been touched before.

There was a time when Tammas, having finished the milking, was bringing the pail across the courtyard and looked up,
full of pride, at his mother, who was standing by the clothes-
line, a day's wash ready to be hung up. And then, cocky-like,
he began to walk with a mincing step, nose high in the air, im-
itating I know not who or what, but risking the full day's milk
supply.

"Tammas, be careful!" his mother called in genuine alarm,
for he was approaching a pile of stones we had cleared out to
make a path.

But it was too late, and Tammas, eyes on the heavens, fell
to the depths of earth, the milk spraying the dirt around him,
only to be greedily licked up by the brown soil. I saw Mrs.
McPherson wring her hands and then raise them to the sky in
sheer exasperation, and I waited for a torrent of abuse to come
from her lips, which the foolish lad deserved, and a good can-
ing to boot, if I had had my way about it.

But as he got up out of the mud, one knee skinned on the
rocks, and tears of hurt pride in his eyes, all he saw was his
mother kneeling down with open arms, waiting for him, and
he ran to her and hid his face in her bosom, while she stroked
his hair in a manner both gentle and fierce, and crooned to

him, "There, there," rocking him back and forth, and never a sign did she give of her irritation, but only of love and acceptance.

"I won't do it again, Mother," he sobbed, for he knew that the loss of a whole day's milk was loss indeed, what with baking and meals and all the rest.

Weak I thought it was at first to act that way, but I'm bound to say that there never was another drop of milk spilled by Master Tammas in all the time I lived with them. And I, who would have belted him, could only marvel at the power of her gentleness.

And there was a time when I got a chill to the very marrow of my bones, and since we were trying to finish cultivating the north field, I kept on working when I should have stopped. The next morning I woke up full of the fever and unable to work. When I failed to appear at breakfast, Mrs. McPherson sent one of the boys, Tammas, I think it was, to inquire about my absence, and after his report, she immediately appeared with a pot of strong tea that she left for me, and her care for me that day was as though I too were a son.

I knew she was strong, for I had seen her driving the animals, lifting huge stones a man would have staggered under, and even managing the ox, but that full day in the byre her presence was all gentleness and lightness. When she lifted my head, so I could manage a swallow of tea, it was a thing of beauty both to see and feel. I dozed the day through, but I realized that many times that day she came to bring a new pot of tea, scalding hot from the kitchen, and fluff the pillow and straighten the rough blankets, though if she thought I was asleep she came and left with a soft and gentle tread.

When I was quite recovered and tried to thank her, she would have none of it. "But Jamie," she said, "you've been such a help to us, it's we should be doing the thanking," and when I took her hand to show my gratitude, she removed it, but not for a moment or two, and with ever so slight a blush on her face.

So I was full of joy when one night, in the presence of the lads, after I had addressed her several times in quick succession as "Mrs. McPherson," she turned to me and said gravely, but with a smile, "Jamie, I don't think you should call me 'Mrs. McPherson' while I call you 'Jamie.' I'd be pleased if you'd address me by my Christian name, and we'll not seem quite so formal and separate from one another."

And although I knew (from looking in the Bible on that first night) what was her Christian name, I replied, "Thank you . . . ma'am. I'd be pleased by that too. And what would you wish that I call you?"

And she, "My Christian name is Moragh, Jamie."

And I, "Thank you . . . Moragh. It will be my pleasure."

Moragh. To ears untuned to Gaelic speech, the name sounds hard and almost harsh, the final "gh" disrupting what might have been only a lilt. But in the highlands and on the islands, it is a sound of music. In some places Moragh can be a word for "heather," and that was likewise a good word for Moragh McPherson, for heather is both beautiful and sturdy, as was she. It can transform a hillside that until its bloom has looked cold and sullen like brackish water, and then one day, ah, there is a sheen of purple loveliness beyond any music, and so soft it seems to be floating just above the earth.

Sheep, in their plodding way, can cross a hillside of heather, and the plant survives their tough hooves, and if a few branches snap, others resist, and the sheep themselves enrich the ground with their droppings. The next season, new shoots spring forth, tender shoots that are protected by mature ones until they too, out of their gnarled and ancient roots, can, with the coming of another season, cast that sheen of floating loveliness across the hills once more.

And that was Moragh. Hardy roots out of generations of forebears tilling that ancient soil, but she the one in whom the beauty had come to flower, so that, hardy though she was, there was a loveliness in the way she walked and the tilt of her head and the care of her speech.

Gaelic uses many words that to Outsiders seem harsh, in order to talk of things gentle and tender. On the islands they sometimes say *mo gradh,* and it too sounds harsh to untrained ears. But it means, my love, my dearest love, my dearest dear, all those things the rest of us take so many words to say. On the islands, *mo gradh* says it all, and its lilt is also a lilt of gentleness.

It was a feeling I was coming to have for her, but I could not give it speech.

Once the plowing was done, we began to watch for the first shoots of new life from the soil. And when the garden and the fields began to produce, the sky was still light at ten o'clock of an evening, the nights themselves were fair, and soon the hay was high toward mowing.

Whatever restlessness I had brought with me from my unknown past had its ugly power diminished by the warmth of the sun, the cool of the nights, the rolling of the hills, the companionship of the lads, and the loveliness of Moragh. I tried not to see the loveliness, for I expected any time that some morning I would wake up with full knowledge of my past, or that a crack on the head would do the trick and I would again find myself the conscious possessor of a wife and children on another island or the mainland. And I still sensed that if I began to give way to my feelings about Moragh, her devotion to Angus's memory, and her island sense of what was "proper," would cause her to rebuff me. So I settled for a companionship that was far removed from love, fearful that to seek more would mean to lose all.

But there was a gradual easing of her stiffness that made me feel, in tiny corners of my being, that she was pleased by my company, as I was by hers. One day on the beach, during a Sabbath excursion with Angus and Tammas, she stumbled over a piece of driftwood and I caught her as she began to fall. She leaned against me for a moment to regain her balance, and sweet the moment was, and then, as always, she took the initiative to move away.

"Thank you, Jamie," she said, as though to close the incident. But then, with an almost mischievous grin, she continued, "I was fair on the way to spraining my ankle. And then you'd have had to carry me the full way home."

And off she was, running down the beach to answer the call of Angus and Tammas, who had discovered a tidal pool teeming with strange creatures.

And I, I stood there and cursed my quick reflex, and wished indeed that there had been a sprained ankle.

Those secret Sabbath excursions. . . . On the Lord's Day, of course, no work was done beyond what was absolutely necessary to feed the cattle and clean the barn. Food was prepared, as much as possible, the day before.

There was no nonsense from Moragh on a Sabbath morning;

it was baths for the boys, a fresh scrubdown, usually with cold water, to prepare them for the service at the kirk. The first Sabbath it was suggested, though not ordered, that a similar preparation would be appropriate for me, though, for reasons I will relate, I chose not to accompany them.

Somewhere in the midst of supervising everyone else through breakfast and scrubdown, Moragh herself would have managed a bath, and would emerge fresh and even radiant at the precise moment they needed to begin the two-mile walk to the village. Dress was sombre, demeanor grave, and the lads looked pained in their stiff clothes.

I was in the awkward position of having no Sabbath clothes, and the even more awkward position that were I to have gone to the kirk, I could have gone only in Angus's suit, which would have been an unnecessary cruelty for Moragh, it being the suit he had no doubt worn for his wedding as well as for the christening of the two lads. So I stayed at home, but I did not work, being sensible to the patterns of the isle.

On one level, Moragh was a deeply committed Presbyterian, strict on Sabbath attendance at the kirk, teaching her sons the Bible stories, and believing with a simple and untroubled faith that Angus Sr. and Fione were safe in the Lord's protection, wherever that might be. Although I never heard her there, I am sure that when they lined out the psalms of a Sabbath morning, she sang with a clear and unaffected purity that must have made even the dire maledictions of King David at his worst have the ring of beauty to them.

But she drew the line on dour Sabbath observance once the service was completed. She insisted, without advertising the fact, that the afternoon and the long evening belonged to her and the children. So they did not walk back to the village for the evening service, nor did they remain indoors and immobile throughout the afternoon, as was often the custom elsewhere on the isle. "The earth is the Lord's," Moragh had learned, "and the fullness thereof," and this meant to her that at least part of the Lord's Day could be spent appreciating the Lord's creation in all its fullness. And this in turn meant to her that to tramp in the glens and even along the beaches was a permissible Sabbath afternoon activity. She reasoned that if there were those who saw them on a beach and reported the fact, the spies themselves would stand convicted of being where they should not have been, and that this was sufficient protection against the development of undue social pressure.

She further protected the excursions by making sure that they ended with a visit to another of the farms where an elderly grandfather looked forward to a Sabbath visit from the two grandsons. This tiny subterfuge transformed the intent of the Sabbath outings from vain and earthly pleasures of the flesh into indisputable works of spiritual mercy that could, if necessary, be offered in celestial courts on high, even if not in ecclesiastical courts below. Of what consequence, or of what possible concern, could it be to prying eyes, if the route to the grandfather's house (a mile or more down the road) should regularly consume four or five miles of circuitous approach through glens, brooks, and beaches?

Since not all folk might understand a logic that was self-evident to her, Moragh and the lads had an unwritten and almost unspoken understanding that the rather complicated nature of their Sabbath excursions was to be discussed only among the three of them, and that to all outsiders they consisted single-mindedly of "going to see the old 'un."

Such was the limit of Moragh's duplicity. In all other things she was without guile. The lads came first; and she, who had to be both father and mother to them, played both roles as fully as she could.

After the first week, when I was left home while the three of them went off "to see the old 'un," I was included in the tiny subterfuge and became a willing conspirator.

They made a kind of believer out of me, those three. For if the Sabbath morning (as I intuited from their comments about the kirk services) presented a dour God, stern of visage and full of demand, the God of the Sabbath afternoons was pure sunshine and brightness and the laughter of the lads and the energy of Moragh racing up the hills with them and then lying down on the sweet grassy meadow full of flowers to catch her breath with them and tickle them slyly with a tuft of sea grass when they were looking elsewhere. Her joy was not so much for herself as for them, and it was a joy that almost brought tears, so selfless it was. Her face was most beautiful, and her eyes most alight, when she was looking into the eyes of Angus Jr. or Tammas, and at those times she was full of a fierce and holy love, and also a pain that she could not look into the eyes of Angus Sr. as well, or with him at the fruits of their shared love.

If the Sabbath were a stormy one, we would still go out, though more directly, to the old 'un's house, and even those dark skies and the pounding surf had a beauty and a grandeur, though always tinged with a terror in her eyes, for I could feel her thinking at such times, though she never said so aloud, "Was it this kind of storm in which Angus's boat went down? And did he fear and suffer and have all manner of pain, or was it over clean and quick?" But then the mood would pass, and she would have a question for Angus Jr., or a hug for Tammas, and her face would be all sunny once again, no matter how fierce the storm.

Over many a Sabbath the lads showed me where the rabbit warrens were, and the places in the rocks along the coast where the plovers hid their eggs, to be looked at but never disturbed, and the shallow pools in the coursing of the brook's descent to the sea where the trout spawned. For hardy lads they had a gentle touch with flowers, and the discovery of a tiny bloom hidden beneath the leaves of a larger plant would draw from them both a sudden intake of breath.

I loved them both, I say directly. And before long I loved their mother too, though that I could not yet say directly. So I loved her indirectly through loving them, hoping she knew that as I became more gentle with them, it was my act of gentleness toward her as well. And I loved the croft and the fields and the bens and the beaches, for all were stamped with the beauty of her presence, and days with a darkness of the clouds were more warm and healing when she was present than days of brilliant sky without her.

And in the same manner that we played on the Sabbath afternoons, so too we worked, and we made of the work a thing of joy, for even hard work shared is work made worthwhile, and when shared with those we love, it is work made holy. So I believe, not because someone taught me with some words, but because, clear and simple, that was the way of it.

Is it with joyfulness that I think of these things? Aye, but with pain too. For it was all too good to last, and when it ended, it was in a way so cruel that I still must ask if the goodness and the beauty of it were worth the tragedy. And I keep answering "Aye."

But I have to keep asking the question, if I am to remember the answer.

It had been a long, hard day of haying, cutting, mounting, storing in the barn, and building sheaves that would stand outside until needed. Much was cut and dried out but not yet piled, when darkness finally interfered with our labors.

Moragh and I were sitting in the living room after supper, dead tired, but with the wonderful fatigue that comes from honest work. The boys, still possessed of an energy I envied, had gone off to see "the old 'un," going directly by road this time, insisting that no one could challenge their innocent "play." Few words were spoken between us. But there was a warmth that had not been there before, and it was not from the unlit fireplace. I heard her humming softly, her eyes closed, her head leaning back against the chair. It was *Vair me o* she was humming, the Eriskay "Love Lilt." And once again I felt her sadness, and there was a sadness in me too, for it was with Angus in her mind's eye that she had always sung it. But this time, as she neared the end of the chorus, she opened her eyes and looked—ever so slightly, but I am sure she looked— in my direction, as she sang, ever so softly, in English now, "Sad am I without thee." I hoped, and was not sure, she was singing to me.

Such had been the rhythm of our chaste courtship, if I may call it that, that I could not ask her directly. But the nature of her glance, shy as it was, emboldened me to rise and, almost for the first time, take her directly by the hand, holding it firmly enough so it could not easily be disengaged, and gently draw her outside into the fast-approaching night. And under the stars, and looking at the darkening day, but looking really at her, though she could not see me doing so, I sang the first verse:

> When I'm lonely, dear white heart,
> Dark the night and wild the sea,

> By love's light my foot finds
> The old pathway to thee.

Did she know that the words were not just the singing of the verse of a song, but were a declaration of love? I did not know at first.

But after we had sung the chorus together and I started to sing the second verse, she joined in, and I knew that the words were now her own, and were addressed to me, and she knew that the words were my own and were addressed to her. We sang to each other:

> Thou'rt the music of my heart,
> Harp of joy, *o cruit mo chridh,*
> Moon of guidance by night,
> Strength and light thou'rt to me.

And so it was that together we sang our love for one another for the first time. And at the end of the singing we were in each other's arms.

For me, months and months of careful control and holding in were suddenly released, and I shook in an ecstasy of love and long-deferred expression, while Moragh, for the first time allowing herself to acknowledge feelings she had until now felt were disloyal, clung to me, trembling all over. Only when the passion had subsided, and we were still standing there clinging to each other were there any words.

"Oh, Jamie," she whispered, "for sure I love you."

And I, "Moragh," and her name was music on my lips, "Moragh," and that was all I could summon, until words came to me that she would understand: "Moragh, *mo gradh.*" It was my declaration of love, uttered in a tongue strange to me, but one she knew and understood.

And for that night, that was the sum of it. We both knew there would be other nights, and I knew it would not be time for us to have each other fully until she had put the memory of Angus to rest so that he would not haunt our lovemaking. And fiercely as I wanted her—for already I felt desire arising in me once again—nevertheless, when she kissed me lightly on the lips and said, in full contentment, "Good night, Jamie lad," and turned to go into the house, making it clear that I was to turn and go to the byre, why I, I too, was content.

And now, bitterly, I rue that feeling of content on the part of both of us, for we never knew each other to the full, even though our love was declared, and as far as all things holy were concerned, we were now husband and wife. No later formalities would have added anything to the fact that we had covenanted together till death do us part. It was our wedding night, a night never consummated.

I went to my solitary cot in the byre, tingling with love and joy and peace. Would I later have sought her out within the house? I will never know. But knowing then what I know now, I would have done so, and would have accepted either her yea or nay, although I would have pleaded for a yea.

I lay on my back on the cot, full of the images of light that the "Love Lilt" had raised in me. "Dark the night . . ." Aye, it had been dark, but it was dark no more, for "love's light" had bathed it in radiance, and by love's light my foot would find a new pathway to Moragh, so that from then on the pathway *to* her would become a pathway walked *with* her. In the light it would be, for she was the "moon of guidance," and she was and would be "strength and light" to me.

An old phrase surfaced from somewhere in me, "from this

time forth, and even forever more." It was a benediction, I judged in my ignorance, and probably about the love of God, but for me it was a seal of blessing on my love for Moragh, and that is all I would ever have needed of the love of God.

And as I lay there, basking in love's radiance, I dreamed and I slept and I woke, and sometimes I slept without dreaming, and sometimes I dreamed without sleeping. But, whether awake or asleep, the light kept increasing in brilliance, as though the very universe were announcing its benediction and blessing, and I was more and more surrounded by bright and dazzling light, always increasing, as though a thousand angels were focusing the brilliant rays of heaven on the tiny byre.

And then, in the midst of all the beauty, there was a thump and a pain across my chest and I was wide awake and tried to sit up, for the brilliance was even more than it had been before. But I could not. The attempt only made the pain more fierce, for I was pinned to my bed by a beam fallen from the ceiling, and the loft above, full of hay, and the thatched roof above it, were all ablaze, not with a heavenly fire of angelic light, as I had thought, but with the earthly fire of some diabolic Lucifer that threatened to destroy not only the barn but me as well. The beam was stout and heavy, hand-hewn by some ancestor of Moragh's. It must have taken half a dozen men to hoist it into place, and it was not about to yield to the frantic importunity of a single pair of arms. It had me pinned, and I could not dislodge it.

And then, above the noise of the fire, I heard the voice of Moragh, shouting as she ran across the barnyard and banged open the door of the byre.

"Jamie!" she screamed, searching with her eyes and voice.

"Are you here? Jamie, there's a fire, there's a fire. . . ." She stopped a moment, out of breath. And then she saw me and she saw my plight. "Oh Jamie," she cried, rushing toward the cot.

Many a night in my imagination I had wished to make love with her in that bed, but never with such futile yearning as at that moment. Her hair was disheveled, her face was taut, and she was wearing a long nightgown and some sort of dressing coat, and her form within them was almost shapeless. But I will remember her longest as she stood in that instant on the edge of terror, as she came toward me, pure and beautiful in her frenzied disarray, ignoring the danger.

Seeing that the longer portion of the beam was on the far side of the cot, she rushed around to it, and started lifting, pulling, sliding, with an extraordinary burst of energy and strength supplied by years of heavy farm work and by adrenaline supplied by the occasion. She soon had me freed from the weight of the beam. But so heavy had been the force of the blow that I was unable to move, even though released from the weight that had held me fast.

Moragh got her arms under mine and pulled me off the bed to the floor. There was a wrenching pain in my chest, and I must have passed out for a moment or two, for what I next remember is her pulling me across the barnyard toward the green mound, which, being slightly raised, and nearly surrounded by stones, was less likely to be engulfed by the flames that were licking more and more ravenously at the hay, both piled up and strewn across the barnyard to dry out. I could hear Angus Jr. and Tammas, shouting to each other as they beat at the flames approaching the house, to keep them from igniting the thatched roof of that building as well.

My legs would not work and my chest was caved in, but Moragh, without my help, got me over to the greater safety of the mound. For just a moment she knelt over me, as though in a posture of love.

"Jamie, love," she whispered, touching me with the gentleness and reassurance with which one would touch a sick child, "don't move. You will be safe here. You will be all right, Jamie, I promise, you will be all right." And after the promise was a benediction: "My love will protect you, Jamie, so stay here while the lads and I put out the fire." She stood up, after kissing my blood-soaked forehead.

During those brief moments the wind had shifted, although we had not noticed it. We noticed it soon enough, however, for it spread the fire though the cut and dried-out hay, and suddenly the green mound was surrounded by a wall of flame.

Moragh was at work in an instant, beating at the flames with her dressing coat, which she had torn off and was using as a flail, all the while stamping on the shoots of flame licking at the grass around us. She managed to beat back the fire on one side and create an opening where, as a result, there was only charred turf, thus providing an exit for me, could I have but walked or crawled there.

I would be safe. Her promise held.

And then the hem of her nightgown caught fire, and in a moment she was all in flames. She ran screaming toward the watering trough.

And that is the last I ever saw of her.

I screamed too, and despite my pain, got up to my feet to follow her, my screams turning into low moans, not of pain for me but of fear for her. Just then, above the crackling of the flames consuming the roof of the byre, came a fearful wailing.

Louder and louder it got as the sound of our own screams diminished. It took me a while to understand what the wailing was.

It was the sound of bagpipes.

I wanted to shout, "Stop playing those damned pipes and come and help us." But all my energy was exhausted by my slowly, painful efforts to get to Moragh through the charred exit in the wall of fire that she had created to save me.

The sound of the pipes got ever stronger, as they seemed to pull me toward them. And at the same time I felt a powerful countervailing force on my arms and legs, as though tiny creatures were trying to keep me from leaving; as though, knowing what I now knew, it were impermissible for me to go elsewhere. I was caught in the midst of a strange tug of war, and I welcomed the assistance of the invisible forces that sought to keep me in Moragh's world. But the pipes were pulling me, drawing me, against my will, to somewhere else. I did not know to where, but I sensed with utter clarity that it was somewhere away from Moragh and Angus and Tammas, away from all that I had come to love. I gladly surrendered to those hands that were seeking to hold me, and, with an immense effort, clapped my own hands over my ears, in an effort to drown out the sound of the pipes, sure that if I could extinguish the sound of their music I could extinguish the steadily increasing power, a power that was calling, calling, calling, "come back, come back."

And then there was a new dimension to my consciousness. I knew I was not only hearing the sound of the pipes, I knew I was hearing the sound of the pipes . . . of Duncan MacDuff.

Duncan MacDuff. . . . Now that was a name unknown on

Moragh's island, and yet I knew it somehow. From where did it come? The past? Another life? Another world? Part of a dream? Slowly I began to recall a face that went with the name, and I remembered words I had heard issuing from the lips of that same face: something about the fact that when the pipes blow, and the Wee Folk are on hand, the past is summoned to the present. And the Wee Folk, as I recalled the legends, would draw people into the past and try to keep them from returning to the present and revealing their secrets. I clasped my hands the harder against my ears, for I realized I was being drawn by those infernal pipes away from Moragh and back into a world I could increasingly remember, a world of Duncan, Hamish, Jennie, and . . . what was it? Ah, yes, a christening in the planning.

I fought desperately, calling on the ties of love to counterbalance the call of pipes, and yielding to the pressures of the force seemingly binding my arms and legs. As though in the vortex of a storm I felt myself whirling, though my feet were still on the ground—or perhaps the world itself was whirling, as time wrenched at itself and dislocated those caught in its tumultuous rearrangements.

Even as the heat of the fire diminished, its brightness increased, rising up from the flames, up, up, into the very sky, so that the stars gradually disappeared, and the sky itself assumed a brightness, as though day had already dawned. So bright it was that my eyes smarted from the unanticipated brilliance, and, involuntarily, I closed them.

And in that moment I heard a voice I recognized, addressing me above the cacophony of pipes and confusion and shattered hopes.

I opened my eyes in response to the summons. The brightness was now the brightness of a summer day. I was standing on a green mound, no pain in my chest, no blood on my face. Close by were the crumbled ruins of what looked to have been a byre, beyond which were the moss-covered walls of a roofless cottage long abandoned and forlorn.

The words penetrated my consciousness, spoken by a familiar voice.

"Come on, Jamie lad . . ."

The Island Now
Hamish and Jennie

"**C**ome on, Jamie lad!"

An irritated Hamish appeared around a bend in the road that had momentarily obscured him from view. "What's been keeping you? It's a full five minutes I've been waiting. Step lively, lad," he admonished, even more commandingly. "When I think of the high tea Maggie Henderson will have waiting. I'm sure they'll not be thinking the best of us if we're late."

As Hamish approached Jamie and looked him full in the face, he terminated his crotchety monologue, to say in a mixture of mystification and concern, "Whist, lad! You look as though you've seen a ghost!"

Jamie was not qualified to pass judgment on the accuracy of this observation or any other. Still blinking his eyes in the face of an unaccustomed brightness, he found that the light was overwhelming a series of dimming recollections he tried desperately to keep in mind—of a farmhouse, of one named (was it?) Moragh, of two lads, of a song in (was it?) Gaelic, of a fire . . .

But he kept losing them. They came and went, returning each time less vividly.

Hadn't there been a fire? The grass around him was not even scorched. Hadn't he fainted? He was standing upright.

Hadn't there been freshly mown hay? The field surrounding him was waiting to be cut.

Hadn't it been nighttime? The sun was only a quarter past noonday.

Hadn't there been a byre, a house, a barnyard? There was no byre, no house, no barnyard, just a few crumbled walls he had often passed before, overgrown with moss and a tangled mass of grass and weeds.

Unable to speak, he looked at Hamish, shaking his head as though to clear it. "I don't know," he finally responded, slowly, "I feel . . . as though I've been in a trance. But that's foolishness," he continued, more briskly now, the Glaswegian business mind taking over, reminding him that aspiring young architects do not have trances. "I must have sat down on the mound to rest a moment, and nodded off without realizing it, for there *was* some kind of a dream, only I can't remember what it was about."

He warmed up to the idea. "That's it for sure, Hamish. I got powerful little sleep last night and I must have dozed off and dreamed. I'm sorry I held you up. But now"—still more briskly— "let's get on with it, and see what Mrs. Henderson has in store for us. I'm famished." And all memory of the dream—if it was a dream—was eclipsed as he stepped off the sithean and back onto the road.

No sooner had they started down the road than there was music in the air, sweet and clear through the valleys and the glens. Duncan MacDuff had stopped only long enough to moisten his lips properly and draw the finest tone from his pipes. At the sound, something stirred in Jamie and then was stilled. He turned instinctively back toward the sithean as though expecting to see something, but there was nothing to see, and he was soon in step with an increasingly impatient Hamish.

Rushing to keep up with the time-conscious parson, Jamie noticed with amazement a few minutes later that they had arrived at the Hendersons' on the stroke of four.

They walked back together at a more leisurely pace in the long afterglow of sunset that makes the Hebrides a place of magic, Hamish carrying a bag with a full dozen scones Maggie Henderson was sending on to Jennie. As they approached the sithean, Jamie again felt a faint stirring that did not quite surface, and he searched the depths of his mind trying to summon whatever lurked there. A combination of sweetness and terror moved toward his consciousness and then receded.

Puzzled, he turned toward Hamish, waving in the direction of the ruins. "Do you know whether someone lived there once?"

Hamish, who in the magic of the afterglow had been privately ruminating on the mystery of divine providence and human freedom, and getting nowhere in reconciling the two, was brought back to his island surroundings with a start.

"Ach, lad, you fair startled me! There must have been a family in there once, but it would have been long ago, as you can see by the state of the ruins. The land must now belong to the Murdochs down the road, for you can see that they've planted the fields. As for the ruins," he speculated, "perhaps there were two byres, back in the days when more of the fields were under cultivation. Sometimes the land does strange things, refusing to yield any crops for many a season, no matter how hard folks try. Strange indeed are the ways of creation and the powers of the Almighty . . ."

With which thought Hamish easily made his way back into renewed speculation about providence and freedom, and the two of them completed the journey in silence, Jamie wondering only why he was so sure there had not been the ruins of two barns.

The narcotic of forgetfulness sustained Jamie through the evening in the living room of the manse. The three of them had their evening tea, augmented by Maggie Henderson's glorious scones. Hamish reported on the baptism rehearsal and the details of the high tea. He even went so far as to speculate that by the look of her Maggie Henderson was already in a family way again. Jennie reported that baby Grace's colic had subsided, though it was right for her to have gone there, sad as she was to have missed the outing to the Hendersons'. The episode at the sithean had by now receded to the minuscule proportions of a slight delay, and particularly since the time had been recouped by brisk walking, neither Hamish nor

Jamie felt it significant enough to report. The tea had a sooth-ing effect, and Hamish's evening prayer had the breath of a benediction on it.

But when Jamie got up to his room, and lay in his bed, sur-rounded by solitude and darkness, benediction was the last thing he felt. A host of troubling images began churning in and out of his consciousness. Aspects of the afternoon dream returned, disjointed but vivid, whirling and confused. There were mixed-up feelings of terror and music and love and there was a fire and there was a song about the music of the heart and there were two boys and there was a smell of porridge and there was a time on the beach with a nearly sprained ankle and there was something about the old 'un and there was a spilled pail of milk and a heavy beam and a name Moragh and a face with the name and joy and pain and light in darkness and feelings of possession and loss.

The images came and went. The most precious were the most elusive.

But there was enough reality even to what was most elu-sive, so that he could almost believe he had been transported into the past and had strange experiences there. With a lu-cidity he found hard to maintain in the darkness, he reminded himself that Duncan MacDuff had been deep in his cups (which was true) when boasting of his power over the forces of time, and that while talk of Wee Folk might be the stuff of legends and faery tales, it was hardly the stuff of everyday ex-periences in the life of Jamie Stuart, graduate with honors of Glasgow University.

A pox on you, Jamie Stuart, he thought. A few fortnights on the isle and and you're already half believing faery tales. Brace up, man!

Only much later did he sleep, fitfully and restlessly. Patches of the dream kept being reenacted. Sometimes he was watching it happen, sometimes he was in the midst of its happening. He heard Duncan play the pipes, he watched Moragh in the barnyard, he felt the touch of her hand when he was ill, and then he was in the byre as she wrestled with the beam; he felt her dragging him to safety, saw her kneeling over him on the green mound, watched her flailing at the burning hay, saw her running in flames toward the watering trough . . . Moragh!

"*Moragh!*" In his sleep he shouted her name as though to summon her. And a moment later, there she was, bending over him with a cool washcloth and soothing words, her touch firm and gentle. Ah! she was real, she was true, it was not a dream at all. Moragh it was, bending over him.

He opened his eyes.

Jennie it was, bending over him, the care of a friend and the efficiency of a nurse beautifully combined in her words and manner.

"Jamie," she soothed, still stroking his brow, "its's all right. It's all right. It's a nightmare you've been having. Screaming and shouting you've been. But there's no fire, Jamie, and you're here with Hamish and me, and all is well. There is no fire, Jamie. The night is cool. So rest, lad. There, there . . ."

She sat down beside him on the bed, held his trembling hand in her strong one, and when his frightened staccato gasps had finally been replaced by long deep breathing, she washed his brow once more with infinite tenderness and something close to maternal love.

Then, it being dark and Jamie asleep already, she leaned over, kissed him gently on the forehead, and departed.

Jamie slept until well past the breakfast hour. Hamish had gone to the village to order paraffin for the kitchen range, and Jamie, having watched his departure from the upstairs window, entered the kitchen quietly to brew a pot of tea before his return. He was not yet ready for company. But Jennie was there, tea already brewed. A potentially awkward moment loomed, but it was resolved by the exchange of a single glance.

Jamie said in that glance, "I'm not so clear about last night except I had a nightmare, but I know that you were with me and that you helped me and I thank you."

And Jennie said in that glance, "Ah, it was nothing, laddie. You were fair upset, for sure, and if you want to talk about it sometime you can do so, but I'll not be forcing you."

The important things having been communicated, they were then free to resort to the less satisfying medium of words, which they devoted to speculating in considerable detail about the likelihood of a storm before evening.

Despite his full discussion of the matter with Jennie, Jamie's mind was not really dwelling on the likelihood of a storm before evening. A turbulence was brewing inside of him greater than could have been unleashed on the whole island by the most vengeful of the storm gods. Every moment, more of the dream was coming into focus, and it had a vividness that made mere dismissal of it harder and harder for Jamie. It *must* have been more than dream. And yet to think of it being more than a dream was to open floodgates that would inundate his heretofore secure universe.

For half the day he wavered in helpless indecision between going back to the sithean to see what he could discover, and staying away from it.

He wanted to go.
He wanted not to go.
At three-thirty he went.

His arrival at the ruins produced only melancholy. The atmosphere was of things past and irretrievable. He skirted the sithean itself, unable yet to cope with memories of the blaze, and made his way to the ruins of what might have been a byre. There was a corner where his cot would have been, from which Moragh would have dragged him that terrible night. And there, just beyond the remains of the wall, was where the trough and the pump would have been, nothing remaining now but a slightly damp area, suggesting that there might once have been a spring. He looked through the tall grass, wondering if there might be some recognizable object of Moragh's or the boys', something that would cry out, "See? It really happened." But then he remembered that it would have had to lie there undisturbed for more than a century and a half.

There could be no such object, and there was not.

He approached decaying walls that would have been the house, intending to enter, and could not bring himself to do so. If he had never really been there, it was futile to pretend to something that was a lie. And if he had really ever been there, it was bitter to stand once again where he had touched her shoulder, where there had been the evening tea and the partings ("Give Jamie a hug for good night, *that's* the lad . . ."), and where he had, on a beautiful night that became fearful, led her by the hand into the darkness to sing with her a song of love.

Yes, the walls suggested the shape of Moragh's cottage, almost enough to persuade him that he had been there. But lu-cidity took over once again, easier to invoke in the daylight than it had been in the darkness, and he realized, ever the architect, that most of the farm buildings on Erinsay were built according to a standard plan, and that the cups of tea he had had in various of them would have planted sufficient impression on his subconscious mind to be recast into a single dream.

He turned away lonely, confused, and sick at heart.

He had started back toward the village when he reflected that he should stand at least once on the sithean; it had, after all, been the place of beginning and ending. It was not Friday, and Duncan MacDuff's pipes were not playing, so there was no reason to expect that there would be any spell surrounding it. He entered its boundaries and felt no tremors. He stamped his foot almost listlessly and said, "Friday, Friday." The air did not change, the sky did not darken or lighten, no hands drew him away, no lads appeared guiding a cow toward her stall.

But memories from the dream focused with such intensity while he stood there that Jamie's listlessness slowly turned to bitterness, and the bitterness rapidly turned to anger. He became, in the space of a few seconds, as one possessed.

"Friday!" he screamed, "Friday! Friday!" and kneeling down, he pummeled the earth, punctuating the sound of his beating fists with "Friday! Friday! Moragh! Friday! Tammas! Angus! Friday! Hear me! Hear me! Come and fetch me! FRI-I-I-DAY!"

But no one heard.

And no one came to fetch.

Let's be done with it, Jamie argued to himself on the way back to the manse: it was a dream and nothing more. An end to all the nonsense.

And nonsense it appeared to be. The notion that at one moment it was 1990, and the next moment it had been 1829, and that he, Jamie Stuart, had been in both moments, was beyond all believing. He began to devise explanations, drawing on the memory of a course in psychology at the university a decade ago: he had lost Annie, and since that was too hard to cope with, he had created a compensatory existence in a fictitious past in which he would win rather than lose the girl.

That worked pretty well, he reflected, up to the time of the fire, and even that could be made to "fit": the fire meant that not even his subconscious yet felt he was worthy of winning such a one as Moragh.

Unpleasant as such a conclusion was, both as a dream and as an estimate of character, at least it *made sense*, much more sense than believing in the power of Duncan's pipes. And Jamie Stuart was one who insisted that things make sense. So he willed himself to put his mind on other things and forget the dream. He planned another hike to the Faery Glen, and even thought of walking the Rutted Road to the Other Side of the island, a place he had not yet visited.

And yet.

There was one thing, and one thing only, standing between Jamie Stuart and full acceptance of the notion that he had simply dreamed a dream. That one thing was Moragh herself.

Jamie could account for dreaming about Wee Folk who were jealous of mortals, and he could account for dreaming about pipes that transported their hearers back and forth in time, for such things had been poured into his ears since the day of his arrival on the island, and his subconscious had clearly been working on them.

But how to account for Moragh? There was the puzzle. There was not a single thing in his past—no friend, no attitude, no art, no poetry, not even the relationship with Annie—that could have influenced his mind or psyche to create a Moragh. He had known almost nothing in his earlier life of the gentleness, the chasteness, the purity, that Moragh embodied; such things could in no way have been his own creation. Her self-giving, her care, the quality of her slowly deepening affection, introduced cadences beyond any melodies he could have conceived. His life and his friendships—even the times with Annie—had been built around competition, strain, and instant gratification. And now, in the light of Moragh's radiance, those values seemed increasingly shabby.

All of which plagued Jamie Stuart with the persistent notion that Moragh must be more than an exercise of his subconscious, that she must be . . . *real*. He could come up with no other word. The beauty, the giving, the sacrifice could be no fiction, no projection out of himself. He could more easily imagine the dissolution of the horsehair stuffed sofa in the Bell's sitting room than he could imagine the ultimate unreality of Moragh and the love he had experienced with her. So although it was impossible to believe that he had been transported through time and space, it was necessary to believe that what had taken place because of that transfer had really taken place, and not just been imagined, and was to be lived for, even died for.

And where was he to go with that?

Was she real?

He must know. He must know, one way or the other. It mattered intensely to him whether there was a real-ness to Moragh, or whether he was the victim of a beautiful but finally painful delusion.

It occurred to him that there must be records on the island, records of births, baptisms, marriages, funerals, that would tell him for sure whether or not there had been a Moragh McPherson in the early nineteenth century. He could check it out. Ah!

Having realized that he could check it out, he wavered once again. Did he really want to know? What if there was no references at all to one Moragh McPherson? That would mean that the most beautiful thing he had ever known was will-o'-the-wisp, unreal, lacking substance. Yet what if he found her name? What would that say about his previously well-ordered world? It was a risk he would have to take.

He went down to the drawing room, where Hamish was catching up on the newspapers that had come on Tuesday's boat. If there were records containing the genealogical history of Erinsay, Hamish would know where they were.

Jamie approached the matter circumspectly.

"Would you be having any more books," he began, "that tell about the history of the island?"

"Aye, there's a book right here," Hamish got up, puffing, and drew down a surprisingly large volume from the shelf, "which tells about the geological history, the early invasions of the Norse and the Danes, and even the Irish, who were here only long enough to leave their name upon the land."

Jamie examined it. In addition to the history, there was a chapter on the birds of the island, which he wished he had had two weeks earlier, and another on the flora and fauna.

"Actually, it's not the flowers or the birds I'm concerned about just now," he explained, handing the book back to Hamish. "It's the folk themselves. Is there any way to find out who was here—just the ordinary people, and which families were in which houses? . . . Just so I can get the feel of the place a bit more," he added quickly, suddenly terrified that from his very general comments Hamish would immediately intuit a specific and almost exclusive interest in one Moragh McPherson.

"Aye," Hamish reflected, concentrating on data rather than intuitions, "there are charts and tables in the cupboard of the kirk hall, of course, though it's been years since anyone asked for them. But," his face brightened, "if it's people you want to know about, and who married whom, and what were the names in the past, well then, lad, there is a marvelous place that is better than all others. I should have thought of it immediately."

Hamish paused to relight his pipe. Jamie noted with passing interest that the tobacco tin was labeled "Parson's Pleasure." The pause turned into an extended silence, as Hamish gave himself single-mindedly to the ritual of first scraping, and then stoking, lighting, and drawing upon his ancient meerschaum. At least, Jamie reflected with mounting impatience, the tobacco seemed well-named.

The clouds of smoke provided a pathway upon which the rays of the morning sun danced their way down to the faded carpet at Hamish's feet.

Feeling like an interloper, Jamie finally intruded into the ceremony.

"Where's that?" he finally asked in a strained voice.

"Where's what?" Hamish's interest had drifted elsewhere during the prolonged ritual. "Ah, yes," he said finally, completing an act of recollection and answering his own question, "the place to find out about the island history. . . . Why, lad, the graveyard, of course! You can find out more from the silent stones, and what they say and don't say, than you can learn from a hundred books. There used to be a small graveyard at

Mulgarry, but the stones are all completely eroded away, and there has been no maintenance for decades. So you can concentrate on ours."

"What a wonderful idea!" Jamie responded, already mentally hustling toward the graveyard. "Of course! In fact," he continued, trying not to appear too eager, "I think I'll just step over there right now." He felt on the edge of discovery. "So if you'll just excuse me, I'll be on my way."

"Ah, but you'll not be leaving until you've had your cup of tea, will you now?"

It was not actually a question on Hamish's part. Or if it was, it was a question that allowed but one response. It was an invitation bordering on demand.

"Jennie," Hamish called in the direction of the kitchen, satisfied that the interrogation had been duly pondered and properly responded to, "will you just put the kettle on the fire? Jamie will be having his elevenses with us."

So for forty minutes, with Jamie in a full dither, there was a sharing of parish news. Ian McDonald, who leads the psalms every Sunday in the kirk, is on the mainland for a fortnight, and while he's away the congregational singing will suffer. The calf born down the road at Sligachan Farm is doing well after a shaky start. Old Mrs. Ferguson's rheumatism is responding to the treatment of herbs that Jennie had suggested. Young Peter MacBride is about to go to the mainland for schooling in engineering, and what for sure will an engineer do on Erinsay? Worst news of all: terrible, terrible rumors are making the rounds once again that the MacBrayne Steamship Line is threatening to change the midweek sailing date from Tuesday to Wednesday, but fortunately it is still only talk and nothing has come of it so far. Still, it is almost a matter for intercessory prayer.

"More tea, Jamie? No? . . . A pity. . . . Well, have a good stroll . . ."

The graveyard was just north of the town, near the kirk, low down toward the sea, in a flat place in a fold between two hills. The sea could be seen from it, so the great, pulsating eternal restlessness of coming and going, going and coming, was always a chorus in the background, while the spray in storm time coated the tombstones nearest the beach with the encrusted reminder of the sea's nearness and its ceaseless energy.

But to balance the restlessness of the sea, there was the restfulness of the low hills, changeable, to be sure, in the long scheme of things, but at a slower pace and one undetected by the human eye. So there was comfort, too, as the curve of the hills sought to enfold the blessed departed, promising them rest until such time as they could hope to be awakened to a new life on another shore of another land where, as the vision in the Apocalypse had declared, there was no more sea.

Jamie made his way there through the town and past the kirk, unlatched the sagging iron gate to the graveyard that was only a partially effective barrier against the intrusion of sheep and stray dogs, and entered. He had stumbled over a few mounds in the taller grass just outside the entrance, where no stones remained to mark the burial plots from far, far distant times, but where there had once been hallowed ground.

Some of the newer headstones were easily decipherable, and, as Hamish had suggested, they told story after story, or at least the broad lineaments of stories a wise one could put together. There in a single row were five McEwans, the parents and three children, all dead within a week of one another, victims of a grippe that had plagued the island in the winter of

1923. And there was the old parson, Hamish's predecessor, who had died in 1948 at the age of—Jamie could hardly believe it—ninety-two; Jamie had heard Hamish say that the old man had preached until a fortnight before his death.

The women, for the most part, had lived beyond their three score years and ten, a hardy breed who frequently survived their husbands. Now and then there was a gravestone with the legend "lost at sea," reminders of a time when more of the islanders had made their living catching fish than, as now, raising sheep. And there were two markers, from the relatively recent past, with foreign names: "Kurt Offenbach" was on one, and "Val Njorsksküng" on the other, though each stone had the same notation, "washed ashore, November 3, 1942." Any islander could have told Jamie that the foreigners were victims of an encounter between a German patrol boat and a Norwegian fishing trawler in the North Atlantic during the war.

Jamie did not linger over the newer stones. He was not deciphering the recent past. He pushed his way, in a mixture of impatience and reluctance, to an older section of the graveyard. On his knees now, he began to examine the inscriptions on the ancient, flat surfaces, smoothed almost clear by generations of wind and rain and slow decay. He worked his way, row by row, toward the farthest wall, beyond which, as if in reminder that death is always triumphant, a new plot was being prepared. Ian McSomething he saw, Callum McDougal, Martha Sloane. But it was not an Ian or a Callum or a Martha he sought, so he kept moving from stone to stone, still on his knees, starting to decipher each one, and shortly forsaking it for the next in line, wanting and not wanting to find the one name he both hoped and dreaded to find.

At the next to the last row the name "McPherson" began

to appear, and Jamie's heart pounded. He was in the midst of the family plot. He stopped for a moment as dizziness overtook him. Ian McPherson he saw, Flora, David, Alison beloved wife of (indecipherable), and on the stone just beside the wall, Mariah . . .

Mariah? It could not be Mariah. That was no Scottish name. He scraped off the lichen and bent lower, shining the flashlight from his rucksack at one side of the stone to create faint shadows across the delicate incisions weathered almost to smoothness. And there, through eyes filling up with the salt tang of the chill air, he saw that "Mariah" was "Moragh," and he read the legend:

Moragh McPherson
widow of Angus McPherson
born Feb. 17, 1796
died by fire
August 19, 1829

He had two instantaneous and simultaneous reactions. The first was elation. There had been a Moragh. She had not been a dream. She had been real. Which meant that their love had been real. The second was devastation. Yes, there had been a Moragh. She had been real and their love had been real, but it was irretrievable, buried beneath the sod for more than 150 years. The proof of her life was the signpost of her death.

Jamie could not bear being in the present without her. He willed that he should be at her side beneath the ground. His will was too weak. Nothing changed.

Still on his knees, he clasped the gravestone, first in silence, and then in weeping. His bitter salt tears fell on the stone, per-fectly at home as they mingled with the wilder salt tears of na-ture, deposited there for a century and a half. He had not wept since his youth, having been taught that it was not a thing for a man to do. And while the weeping was an anguish, it was also, in a strange way, a first step toward healing.

And then, as the mist and the fog had kissed the stone year after year, decade after decade, Jamie too, following their example, kissed the stone. It felt strangely warm. He experienced the closest possible communion with the dead.

Spent, he finally arose, old and stiff now, and walked slowly back to the manse. Complaining of a chill, he went directly to bed. For a time he needed to experience the least possible communion with the living.

Only much later, when he was stronger and younger, did Jamie Stuart return to the graveyard. It was a difficult and necessary pilgrimage. And there, telling him many stories both sad and beautiful to hear, were the names of others on the island.

But it was over the McPhersons that he lingered longest. Angus Sr. and Fione were there sharing a common headstone, and in the next row were Angus Jr. and Tammas, both of whom had stayed on the island and lived to a fullness of years and had their own wives and children.

He must carry through to the end. So next day Jamie borrowed the keys to the cupboard in the kirk hall where the ancient town records were kept, timing his request to coincide with Hamish's departure to visit the ailing Mrs. Ferguson. Jamie wanted to conduct his exploration with no one peering over his shoulder or looking too directly into his eyes.

After locating the appropriate folio volume and blowing the dust off it, Jamie made his way back in it to the year 1829, looking for a record of the funeral and burial of one Moragh McPherson. His search was rewarded. After a sparse accounting of the basic statistical information about the funeral (time of day, number present, officiating clergyman, Scripture read, and so forth) the keeper of the archives had recorded some further information to explain the sad occasion.

Deciphering the fair script of the clerk with difficulty, for the ink was faded and browned, Jamie made out:

"Moragh Duffie, born in 1796, was married in the kirk on June 20, 1812, to Angus McPherson, born in 1791. They had two surviving children, Angus and Tammas, a third child, Fione, dying [indecipherable, possibly "stillborn"]. Angus, Sr. died at sea during the great storm of February 18–21, 1826 and [indecipherable]. In 1829 at harvest time, fire broke out at night in the byre of the Widow McPherson's croft and swept over the surrounding fields. The Widow McPherson was consumed by the flames, her body being found next morning near the green mound beside the byre. Her two sons, Angus and Tammas, have been claimed for raising by Jean Dalgleith Duffie, spinster, sister of the Widow McPherson."

Jamie turned the page. There was one more entry.

"A hired hand, name unknown, is presumed to have perished also, though no remains were found."

Elation and devastation continued to wrestle for possession of Jamie's soul.

His life with Moragh had been real and their love had been

real. His life with Moragh had ended and their love could not be recaptured.

The compelling reality that for once in his life there had been love and tenderness and deep commitment would buoy him up, only to be destroyed by the equally compelling reality that it was no more.

It was a puzzle that he had taken no recollection of his own world into Moragh's world. The best he could do with that was to conclude that the "past" that he had brought to Moragh's world was a "future" in her world that would not happen for 170 years. No wonder he could not "remember" in her world things that had not yet taken place there. This did not mean that such remembrance was impossible (Jamie Stuart had by now decided that nothing could be relegated to the realm of the "impossible"), but it did at least mean, he reflected grimly, that while some folk might have the second sight, Jamie Stuart was not among them. And even he could realize that for the likes of Jamie Stuart the second sight would have been difficult to handle.

There was a reverse fact for which he felt the same combination of elation and devastation, which was that although he did not "remember" the present when he went into the past, he did remember the past when he returned to the present. Had it not been so, he would now be oblivious to the memory of Moragh, something for which to give thanks, even though a terrible price was attached to such knowledge. And while it would be frightening to know things that had not yet happened, it was reassuring (if again a source of both elation and devastation) to know things that had already happened. That gave just a bit of stability to a world that was otherwise gyrating wildly around Jamie Stuart.

He had not known Annie in Moragh's world. Of course not.

But he had known Moragh in Annie's world. Of course.

Annie. For the first time in many days and many nights he thought of Annie. As he reflected on his love for Annie in the light of Moragh's love for him, he felt something only dimly sensed in the previous experience of Jamie Stuart. He felt something akin to shame. Others, more sternly, might have called it guilt, and Hamish, had the matter been broached to him, might have called it sin. But whatever it was, it was a new feeling for Jamie Stuart, and one with which he was uncomfortable.

Even putting the best possible interpretation on his actions—an exercise to which Jamie Stuart brought a lifetime of experience—he saw with increasing clarity that he had exploited Annie. He had lived on the assumption that the firm came first, and that she came second. Which meant that if the firm came first, *they* came second. Which really meant that she came third. He had demanded the immediate gratification of sex without the long-term commitment of love, thereby denying her what she wanted most, which was just the opposite— the immediate commitment of love and the long-term gratification of sex.

He had insisted that she be available when his whim and instincts dictated, and had been irritated and even angry when she failed to conform to schedules of his devising. He had interpreted the pregnancy as her fault, and had tried every possible way of avoiding responsibility or facing the consequences. And his only sustained proposal for dealing with the pregnancy had been a demand that took no account of her feelings or her wishes. No wonder she had wanted no more of him.

What kind of a future was he to build from all of this? He could not go back to Moragh, who was dead. Was he to go back to Annie, who was still alive? He sensed that resolution did not lie in the past, anyway, but in the present and the future, for he clearly had unfinished business in the present, and only out of completing that could he shape a future: he had left Annie bereft and unhealed, and that wrong must somehow be righted.

He saw Moragh's face and then Annie's face in something akin to a vision. And although he knew that Moragh was gone and would not return in the flesh, he sensed that she had left him something that would never be gone and could always return. She had left him a sense of caring, a gift that was new and indestructible.

As he watched Moragh's face, he felt that her lips were almost forming words, words he both wanted and did not want to hear. Something like: when you're up to it, Jamie, go back to her. Tell her you're sorry. Tell her that whatever happened between the two of you, you want to make right what became so wrong.

Yes, Jamie Stuart did want to hear such words, and was half formulating them himself, for his spirit was now in a deep kinship with Moragh's.

No, Jamie Stuart did not want to hear such words, for the cost of heeding them would be high. The humiliation, that was the nub of it. To acknowledge that he had been wrong would not only be a new experience but a frightening one, since it would involve thinking first of the welfare of another, and only second of the welfare of himself. Unless—and it was the memory of Moragh that furnished the clue—unless in first seeking the welfare of Annie, he might find his own welfare provided for.

A gull floated by the window, motionless for a moment before being carried out of sight. Like that soaring gull, wafted and supported by invisible breezes, Jamie's spirit soared in a way it never had before.

Gulls. How clumsy and awkward they look standing on the ground, with gawky feet and protruding beaks, inert and lumplike. But once airborne, how full of grace, feet tucked away out of sight, powerful and free when sustained not by their own power but by the power of the wind.

Jamie felt like that now. Alone and self-contained, he too was lumpish and stupid. But the very breath of Moragh lifted him, soaring, sustained by her power, reaching for undreamed of things. It was a goodness. A terrible goodness, he realized, when he saw that what she had done for him he must do for Annie. But he was content.

"Thank you," he said almost reverently, "thank you, *mo gradh.*"

Going down the stairs two at a time, Jamie found Hamish and Jennie in the drawing room in front of the wireless listening to the Home Service. Jennie was making the first stirrings toward the kitchen for the preparation of the evening meal.

"You'll not be needing to go to the kitchen tonight, Mrs. Bell," Jamie announced formally and firmly. "The three of us will be going to the hotel for dinner."

"And why would that be, Mr. Stuart?" Jennie replied on cue, drawing herself up to full height at the very thought of being ordered about in her own household.

"Because I say so, Mrs. Bell," Jamie responded from *his* full height, which gave him the advantage over Jennie by a foot at least. "For my last dinner on the island I wish you both to be my guests, as I have been yours for so many weeks. For I've business to attend to on the mainland, and I go there on to-morrow's boat."

Hamish took the announcement at face value and made supportive sounds of dismay, both at the thought of Jamie's departure from the island and at the thought of his having to go back to an office routine.

But Jennie, after a cloud had passed over her face, heard something deep beyond the words themselves, something in the tone of voice, and knew there was healing in it.

"If that's the way it is, we'll miss you, lad," she said. "But Jamie," and her voice went all soft and was full of a maternal love, "I'm powerful glad for you."

Not touching, they embraced.

The Mainland Now
Jamie Stuart and Annie Cameron

t was not an easy thing for Jamie Stuart to ring up Annie. It was not an easy thing because there was contrition in his heart, and contrition denied him the self-assurance with which he had previously controlled their conversations. He was no longer the strong purveyor dictating terms; he was the weak supplicant pleading for terms. He was no longer uttering a decisive "I'll be around at six sharp; be sure you're ready," but rather a hesitant, "Please, Annie, would you let me talk with you just *once*? . . . No, it's not for saying over the telephone. . . . Annie, please, just name a time and I'll be there." Not very often had Jamie Stuart said "please."

Nor was Annie eager for the encounter. Having felt, correctly, that Jamie Stuart had finally shut her out of his life, she had determined for the sake of dignity and sheer survival to do the same, and was making rather a success of it. Why should she let him open up old wounds that were beginning to heal? So her first inclination was to keep the case of Stuart v. Cameron off the docket.

But Jamie was importunate. "Some things have happened, Annie, and I need to talk with you. I only want to set things right so we don't leave the past an ugly sore."

Annie, with a caution borne of long experience in dealing with Jamie Stuart, sensed a trick and searched for what lay beneath the request. At the same time she realized that although the wound was beginning to heal, the scar would not disappear unless the wound were fully cleansed; if not, the "healing" would do no more than guarantee a yet deeper infection. So, still wary and still hurt, she agreed to a meeting on the following evening.

Jamie spent a restless day, sitting in the public library, walking in the park, sifting and sorting matters that were still new to him. When his resolution or his clarity wavered, he conjured up a vision of Moragh, and once again heard her saying to him, "Tell her you're sorry, Jamie. . . . Tell her you want to make right what became so wrong." The vision sustained him; the desire to set things right with Annie was the right desire.

But since the experience was new, he had few words with which to communicate it, and when a nervous Jamie finally entered the flat of an equally nervous Annie, the awkwardness they both felt made his task even more difficult. Consequently, the initial part of the evening was not notable for the clarity of Jamie's presentation.

There was, however, undeniably a new tone behind Jamie's words, and Annie sensed it. It was a tone at once humble and caring, characteristics never previously applied to the tone of Jamie Stuart's speech, nor to Jamie Stuart himself, for that matter. And his tone was more important than his words, which had a tendency to tumble and trip and land clumsily upside down more often than not. But the gist of the words, turned right side up again, was clear, and this was the sense of it: "A thing has happened, Annie, a thing I can't yet really understand or talk about. But it has shown me that I treated you wrongly and that to let the wrongness go unattended only makes it worse. I can't undo the wrong—it's *there* and it happened and I can't make it unhappen—but I can tell you now that I wish I hadn't been that way, and that I'm sorry and that I ask you to forgive me if you can. It's a heavy weight hangs over me, and it can't be lifted without your help. I've no claim on you for this, considering how badly I treated you, but I ask it of you even so, deep from in my heart."

Long before the complicated recital had been concluded there were tears in Annie's eyes, for the fumbling and the stumbling added authenticity to the penitential outpouring of the one who was usually so debonair and self-assured. Her response was clear, though before it was done it led in a direction neither had anticipated.

"Up to now," Annie responded, "there's been no forgiveness in my heart, I'll have to tell you plain, Jamie Stuart. It's angry I've been, and hurt and lost.

"But when I hear you talk just now, and even more when I look at you, it's for sure that you're a changed man, and no two ways about it. Tonight is no 'trick' like the old Jamie used to play to get his way with Annie. I'd never have thought it possible, but it is possible, so I find it in me to say now that I bear you no grudge, and it lifts my heart to say so, as you said it would lift your heart to hear it. I'm not so experienced in the forgiving business, Jamie, and though it's powerful hard, I feel right now that it's powerful easy as well."

And here their surprise began, for, without having anticipated it, she went on, "And if it comes to that, Jamie Stuart, I guess it was to go both ways. For sure as we're sitting here, if it takes two to make a quarrel, so likewise it takes two to set it right. And although it never seemed so until now, I guess the fault was mine as well as yours. Stubborn I was, loving you so much, and wanting one way or the other to have my will over yours, and then not being willing to talk to you after it all came apart.

"So I'll likewise be asking you to pardon me, and then we'll both be able to begin again."

Whatever he had been prepared for, Jamie had not been prepared for this. Forgiveness, he reflected, was a complicated business.

So there was a mutual pardon, given and received by each, and deep chords were touched for which there are no ordinary words or voices, and so are better left unsaid, unsung.

It was Annie who resumed the conversation after a long and healing silence.

"I'm at peace with myself now, Jamie, and I feel there's peace between the two of us as well, which there hasn't been for many a month. And for that I'm grateful to you, Jamie.

But there's another matter we must talk about. For it's with this kind of peace, Jamie lad, that we must leave it between the two of us. When you left, and you so angry, and I so full of hurt, I closed the door on you, as it seemed you'd done to me. And when there was no word for days and weeks and months, and your office said you were on leave and holiday, and I was left full in the dark, I heard your message loud and clear: there was no part of your heart left for me, just as there was none of mine left for you. So I said to myself, 'If there's one thing I won't do, it is to wait for his return and be rebuffed again,' as it seemed to me. 'No man is going to destroy me that way,' I said.

"So, Jamie, the long and the short of it is, I've met another man. He's gentle, and he loves me, and he knows about the wee one that didn't come, and loves me even so. And he's asked my hand, and I've said yes, and I'm not about to reconsider that promise. I know it's been fast, but that's what's happened, Jamie lad, and I love him and I plan to marry him."

And then, more softly: "I'm sorry if that hurts you, Jamie, and I'm sorry to be the one as brings the hurting. Hurting and loving seem to be so close together, and perhaps I need to ask your forgiveness for that, too."

And Jamie, after a long silence, Moragh's face before him, said, "No, you needn't be asking my forgiveness for falling in love, when I turned my back on you for so long. I'll be honest that it's not so easy to hear what you've just been saying. But there is one thing I must say to you as well." And with a certain vision before his eyes, Jamie continued: "If you would know the truth, part of what brought me here tonight is that I needed to tell you that I've also loved another. But the one I loved is dead." He stopped for a moment and then continued reluctantly, when Annie's face went all soft. "She always was dead, though I didn't know it."

Puzzlement replaced softness on Annie's face. "Jamie, I don't understand *that*," she started to interrupt, but he continued, and now he was the one for whom softness was the word.

". . . Nor do I really understand what I'm saying, save that it's true, though that's all I can rightly say about it. I loved her, and she is dead. But her love was a giving and not a grasping love, and she taught me, by never a word but always by who she was, that what we love we sometimes must risk losing, and must let go. And since I cannot have you, I let you go to this . . ." He fumbled for a name he did not know.

"Duncan . . ." she prompted, drawing a momentary look of utter astonishment from Jamie, which relaxed when she finished, ". . . Anderson."

". . . this Duncan Anderson," he continued. Then for a moment the softness was replaced by the old fighting Jamie. "I just hope he knows what a lucky bastard he is, although that's hardly a word for me to use about the man you'll marry."

Annie set him at ease. "I called *you* that once, Jamie Stuart, in a time of anger, and I'm fair ashamed of myself for having done so."

The exchange broke through the gravity of the situation, and they were suddenly all smiles as Jamie said, "Well, Annie, at least your taste in men seems to be consistent. And maybe, seeing we're so much alike, I'd like the fellow after all."

It made the leave-taking easier. Jamie kissed her, not roughly as he often had before, but gently. It was not a kiss of grasping but of letting go. She held him, not fiercely as she often had before, but tenderly; it was a drawing close for the purpose of drawing away. There were the beginnings of some tears, but each took care not to notice them in the eyes of the other, and Jamie had turned and departed before they became a problem for either one.

Jamie reached the street conscious in the midst of pain that something very good had just been done. He knew that Annie was now free for a new life, and that her chapter with him had been creatively concluded. He knew that the gift Moragh had given him had been used in ways that would please her. He knew, however, dimly, that through the pain of one, healing can come to another.

For a moment, the beauty of their exchange transformed the drabness of the Glasgow streets, which came alive as though with the glory of the celestial city.

And then, as suddenly as the traffic light before him changed from "Go" to "Stop," there was no more glory. There was only drabness.

He realized in pain and in fright that he was unalterably alone. Two gifts had been given him in his life, one named Annie and one named Moragh, and they had both been withdrawn. Moragh's death had saved him, which was an enduring truth. But Moragh's death had not saved her, which was another enduring truth. He was left with the unchangeable facts that Moragh was dead, and that while Annie was alive, she was dead to him. He had given her some kind of blessing, and he had received a blessing in return, but once the brief moment of exaltation had passed, there was nothing left inside him but emptiness.

The emptiness inside was suddenly and starkly an account of everything outside as well: empty warehouses; empty buses filled with empty people; an empty city teeming with empty individuals not reaching out, not touching, not caring; an empty world spinning out its orbit in an endless uncaring ever-echoing space.

He felt a part of all that he surveyed, and was not sustained.

By the time the light had changed again from "Stop" to

"Go," Jamie had a firmly fixed agenda for eluding the emptiness. He crossed the street, entered the Fowler's Pigeon, and spent the evening trying to erase that taste.

If it had "worked," Jamie never knew about it, for his memory had only just begun to function again. Brutal shafts of light assaulted his eyelids, relentness piledrivers working their way through resistant covering. For a few moments he tried to fend them off, first with his hands and then by putting his head under the blanket. But nothing helped.

Some Good Samaritan had gotten him back to his flat, he decided, for the surroundings began to assume a degree of familiarity. There was his armchair, yonder the closet, beyond that a door to the kitchen, near at hand his clothes in a mass on the floor.

Clothes. A thought occurred to him. Not all Samaritans are good. Maybe this one had cleaned him out. The trousers were almost within reach. With great effort he drew them toward him. Sure enough. No wallet. The bastard. But then a corner of the wallet came into focus under the pile of cloth that had once been his shirt. Adjusting his eyes very slowly and with considerable pain, he brought the wallet into focus, noted that there were still some bills in it, and gradually deciphered a receipt, duly signed by "G. Harris," proprietor of the Fowler's Pigeon, itemizing the consumption of seven double whiskies for Jamie, and two rounds of drinks for the house. Judging by the size of the claim for reimbursement of the latter item, a considerable portion of the male population of Glasgow had been the beneficiaries of an unaccustomed generosity.

He made his way to the bathroom turned on the cold water tap, cupped his hands, and dowsed his face, a necessary rite of passage back into a world he loathed.

The action cleared Jamie's head. The world *was* loathsome. He could not face fifty years of loathsomeness. The future held no charm. Trapped.

And then, seeping into his consciousness, but lurking for a while just beyond reach like a presence sensed but not seen in the dark but slowly assuming recognizable form, came another thought: the future holds no charm, but maybe the past still can . . .

Was the past forever closed off to him? He had been there once; could he not return? He knew the way, and if he could get the proper help, perhaps he could cross the threshold once again. Was there only one such opportunity in a lifetime? Certainly nothing Duncan had said would rule out the contrary. Perhaps if he went back to Erinsay he could make a pact with Duncan, and return to the world of Moragh.

He knew nothing of how such things worked. Even if he could negotiate an agreement with Duncan, was there any assurance that he would be returned to the same point in time? If he were, though, he would fight to keep the fire from consuming Moragh—whatever that might mean about the gravestone and the town records. And if he were too late for that, and she could not be saved, then he would struggle to find a way to raise Angus Jr. and Tammas, lavishing on them his love for her—whatever that might mean about Jean Dalgleith Duffie, spinster, who had been "assigned" the task of raising them. And if he were deposited in the past long before, or long after Moragh—well, he would come to terms with that and make a new life, taking care only to stay away at all times from green mounds. And if he got back there, and remembered nothing at all about who he had been, as seemed likely on the evidence so far at his disposal, well, it was a gamble and by God, he would take it.

It was very confusing. In fact, there were only two things about which there was no confusion, and he was very sure of both of them: first, Moragh was somewhere in the past, and second, Duncan was his means of getting there. Yes, it was a gamble, an immense gamble. Yes, he was prepared to take it.

He said to an invisible presence: "I'll not be without you, Moragh. So to the island I'll go once again, and then with Duncan's help, I'll make my way to where you are. I'll seek you out through all the corridors of time until I find you, once again, and then, *mo gradh*, there will be no parting us, any more."

A strange sort of peace settled over Jamie Stuart in the succeeding days as he carried out a number of necessary tasks.

First of all, he asked Mr. Ferguson for an indefinite leave of absence from the firm of Abercrombie and Ferguson, Ltd., beginning two weeks hence, citing ill health and "personal problems" as the reason for the request.

Mr. Ferguson was not enchanted. He had banked on the fact that the time on Erinsay would "shape up young Stuart," as he put it, and leave him "fit as a fiddle," as he also put it. He was, indeed, personally affronted by Jamie's request, signaling, as it did, the failure of his own handsome gesture to Jamie just a few months earlier.

At last he grudgingly conceded a maximum of three months' leave, during which all salary (" . . . *and* benefits, Mr. Stuart") were to be terminated. Jamie, whose backup position would have been a simple resignation, or an even simpler walking out one afternoon and never returning, acquiesced to Mr. Ferguson's counter-offer, since he was sure that he would have both negotiated and consummated a pact with Duncan MacDuff long before three months had elapsed.

Next, he terminated the rental of his flat thirty days hence and paid the forfeiture fee for early closing of a tenancy agreement that still had eighteen months to go.

He set up a trust fund for Annie, and left instructions with his solicitor that it should be delivered to Mrs. Duncan Anderson on the morning of her wedding, whenever that should be.

He withdrew his remaining funds from the Royal Bank of Scotland, keeping only enough cash on hand for rental to the Bells, incidental expenses in the next month, and standing Duncan MacDuff to whatever number of drinks might be required to persuade him to play the pipes of a Friday afternoon.

He surprised the pastor at the local kirk (a building he had never entered) by offering his furniture for sprucing up the youth center in the parish hall, though he did suggest, in an attempt at levity the dour cleric did not appreciate, that the bed might be omitted from the recreational facilities offered to the youth of Glasgow in their newly festooned room.

Intermittently, he wondered what to do with his sailboat. Should he sell it, give it away, or lend it indefinitely to an unsuspecting friend?

And then he had an inspired idea. He would sail it to Erinsay. Though he had never sailed through quite so much open water before, he was sure he could manage. It was a decision that solved several problems for him. It solved the problem of the disposal of the boat. It gave him a perfect, and even verifiable, way to account for his forthcoming departure. ("I'm going off to sail amongst the islands for a few months and put things back together.") And it satisfied romantic longings from his youth to sail out over the edge of the horizon. He bought nautical charts and worked out a route from Glasgow to the open sea. He figured on a fortnight all told, depending on the winds, to make it from the Glasgow port down past the isle of Arran and the Mull of Kintyre and then on to Erinsay, and he charted a course that would guide him from the last lighthouse on the westernmost point of the mainland until the familiar shape of Ben Erinsay greeted him over the horizon.

And then! On it would be to Duncan MacDuff, and an escape from the certainty of an unendurable present into the possibility of a healing past.

There was a small party the night before he left, and one friend, several sheets to the wind, tearfully begged to go with him. When it was clear that her pleadings were falling on deaf ears, she finally said, "Well then, Jamie lad, I'll be a-waiting your return."

Jamie gave her wise counsel. "Don't," he advised.

The Island Now
Moragh McCallum

eaving his way through a maze of anchored vessels at about five in the morning, Jamie was filled with exhilaration. Given a good breeze—and the day promised to be fair—he would arrive at Erinsay by late afternoon. Hamish and Jennie were expecting his arrival, and he relished the thought of high tea before seeking out Duncan in the pub and starting to lay a groundwork that in the course of time would lead to Duncan playing the pipes at a certain time of a Friday afternoon when the Wee Folk would be on hand and, by prearrangement, Jamie would be on the sithean stamping and shouting "Friday . . ."

But along with the exhilaration went apprehension, and it was threefold.

First, what if old Duncan simply got his back up and said no? Or agreed to play but only at a time of his own choosing? Or kept postponing a decision? Or extracted too much information from Jamie and blabbed to the other islanders after all those whiskeys?

Second, what if he got back into the past, and having lost his "memory" in the process, never did find Moragh McPherson, or could not recall her? He had resolved to place all sorts of notes and letters to himself in his clothing to try to bridge the gap.

Third, even worse; what if the whole scheme simply didn't work? What if Duncan cooperated to the full, and then Jamie stamped and stamped and shouted and shouted while Duncan played and played, and nothing, absolutely nothing, happened? Maybe, Jamie was forced to concede, one gets only a single chance to dwell in the past. But that, as he had reflected before, was the chance he was willing to take.

And then the sailboat passed his final land's end, and the tiny harbor was left behind, and he entered a long stretch of open sea, the last that lay between him and the leeward side of Erinsay. His sail, no longer sluggish, filled out, and he soon tacked into a strong headwind. The boat, its sail trimmed, trembled under the invisible power propelling it, and the spray began dashing up over the bow. The sea was deep blue and the whitecaps a brilliant contrast, their spray creating tiny rainbows as the bow cut through them and dispersed their symmetry, after which they reformed behind the vessel, chastened by its wake.

Jamie set the tiller and found that without a conscious willing of it, exhilaration had overcome apprehension. He was on his way to the land where, with Duncan's help, he would find his way back to Moragh, and, once there, would guard himself against ever standing again on a sithean and being lured back from a full past into an empty present.

His circumstances reminded him of a passage about halfway through Sheppherd's big book on Erinsay, which he had tracked down in a secondhand bookshop in Glasgow and bought to sustain him during the solemn moments of "putting his affairs in order." He pulled it out now from the waterproof pouch, along with the tins of tobacco he was taking to Hamish. (One of them, "Presbyterian Mixture," was certain to be well received, but he felt less sure of Calvinist approbation for the other, which was called "Three Nuns.")

Where was the passage? Ah, bottom of page 341, and all of page 342:

"There is a tune in the metrical Psalter often sung on Erinsay called 'St. Columba' after the Irish warrior who settled on Iona after a brief stop on Oronsay, and from there Christianized the Scottish isles and the western mainland. The words are usually those of the twenty-third psalm, the one about the shepherd and the sheep, which is a good image for Erinsay, for of sheep there are many thousands, and if the care that our shepherds expend on even a single lamb who falls behind is a picture of the care of God for the very least, then we know for sure that we are well provided for.

"But sometimes music evokes images we do not create or control, images that reappear, unbidden, when the melody is heard. And the tune 'St. Columba' is not so much for me the land and the sheep as it is the sea that surrounds the land and the sky that broods above them both. Perhaps it is because Columba came to the isles in a tiny coracle, and a stern eye would have been needed on both sea and sky at all times, else no coracle would ever have made it across the open sea from Ireland.

"However that may be, whenever I hear 'St. Columba' in the Erinsay kirk, it's offshore I am, looking southwest in the late afternoon. It's a gray blustery day, so the music tells me—gray sky, gray sea, gray gulls, the world all reduced to monochrome, save for the skuddering whitecaps that are dancing all over the sea, and reminding me, along with the chill on my face and the salt on my tongue, that it's a fair wind has come up and that I'd best be making for land.

"But it's more the music says than that, for through that gray and heavy overcast there comes, every now and then, a piercing shaft of light, and the sun bursts through the gray wool blanket the sky has tucked around the earth, and a tiny slice of the sea or land is suddenly full of a silver glory. They dart around, those shafts of light—now here, now there, and sometimes, in the lavish moments of nature's bounty, both here and there simultaneously, and then, nowhere at all, only to gain entrance again far off toward the horizon, as a weakness in the blanket tears apart and the light behind it is once more displayed.

"So when we sing 'St. Columba,' it always calls to mind those moments when shafts of silver fleck the darkness, and the gulls are crying and swooping and riding on the currents of air, and the wind is keen and the smells are salt-like, and I find, deep within me, how good it is to see such things and know that life can be encompassed by such wild and fearsome beauty."

In a few hours Jamie was taking his sights from the tip of Ben Erinsay, now in view on the horizon, and he steadily narrowed the distance between himself and his goal, nourishing himself at high noon with the sandwiches and thermos of tea he had prepared while still tied up in a tiny port, dividing up the rest of the unfinished loaf into small bits for the few gulls who had followed him all the way in hopes of just such bounty.

And then, around the spit of land, he sailed into full view of the tiny Erinsay harbor, its pier jutting out past the rocks. It was high tide, so Jamie maneuvered his craft close to land, tying up on a post of the pier down which a ladder had been constructed.

He saw not a soul while he secured his landing, and that surprised him, for even though this was not a day when the boat from the mainland was due, there was always a small crowd hanging around the pier, tidying things up, or painting the metal braces against the constant encrustation of the sea, or just waiting for the moment when someone would be moved to tell a tale of the past. Puzzled, Jamie climbed the ladder, leaving his belongings on board for the moment, and made his way along the path toward the village. Still not a living soul. It was as though Duncan had gotten all the island folk to stand up on a huge sithean and had transported the whole kit and caboodle back a century or more into the past.

Pulling him from his reverie came a sound of singing from the kirk. Good Lord, he thought, smacking his forehead in dismay, am I a whole day off in my reckoning, and have I gotten here on the Sabbath? They won't take kindly to a long sea voyage on the Lord's Day. But he reassured himself by observing that it was on toward 5 P.M., and he knew that heaven and earth and all of Erinsay would pass away before the morning act of divine worship could be changed from the sacred hour of eleven o'clock of a Sabbath morn and held at a different time. So it's not the Sabbath, he reasoned. But what's going on? A wedding perhaps?

As the road wound along the nether side of The Rise, he temporarily lost both sight and sound of the kirk. When it came in sight again, he understood why the pier had been so deserted. Clearly the whole population of the island had been at the kirk, for they were coming out now, filing up the road to the north in procession. Dressed in somber finery, they were moving slowly and silently.

"What *is* this?" Jamie wondered, drawing closer but not too close, for he wanted to keep some distance since his sailing garments were singularly out of phase with the present garb of the islanders. The head of the procession got to the crown of the hill beyond the kirk, and he saw that six men, dressed in black, were carrying a coffin on their shoulders. The singing had been at a funeral and the procession was moving—where else?—toward the graveyard.

Now Jamie drew closer to the rear of the procession, for curiosity had outbalanced his sense of the incongruity of his dress. He wanted to rush up to someone near the end of the line, if only for a moment, and ask, "who died?" But the silence of the folk, broken only by the shuffling of their feet and the occasional cry of a gull, was not to be violated. Speech, on that silent, solemn journey, would have been a desecration. So he began to check over the faces. Hamish, of course, was in the lead. And there, not too far back, was Jennie. Callum was helping to carry the coffin along with Angus, Ian, and three others whom he could not at a distance identify, since their backs were to him. He saw Alison MacDuff up near the front, walking with Jennie, and the children of the isle, only a few of whose names he knew, throughout the crowd, all uncomfortable in their starched clothes and prickly underwear. Though their backs were to him, he could imagine their faces fixed with a rigid solemnity, as though a temptation to laugh or even smile was being forcibly restrained.

The procession grouped itself around the open grave—the first, Jamie noted, in the new section of the cemetery. Since most of them still had their backs to him, he had to give up his eerie game of trying to eliminate further candidates for election to death.

And so, standing apart but within earshot, since the wind was blowing in from the sea, he picked up most of the words that Hamish read from his little black book:

"I am the resurrection and the life. . . . Man, who is born of woman. . . . Yea, though I walk through the valley of the shadow of death. . . . O grave, where is thy victory?"

And then, after Hamish had led in prayer, Jamie saw the coffin being lowered into the ground, and by straining he heard the words (for the wind had shifted once again): "And so we commit into the Lord's care and protection, in sure and certain hope of the resurrection, the body of our beloved brother, Duncan MacDuff . . ."

With the door shut, Jamie sat in his room at the Bells', staring with unseeing eyes at a future now inconsolably bleak. A single sequence had become clear to him: no Duncan Mac-Duff . . . no return to the past . . . no Moragh . . .

His first impulse had been to march straight back to the pier, climb aboard his sailboat, clear the harbor, set a course due west, and keep on sailing until the sea claimed him.

The impulse was short-lived. Jamie was not really one for the grand gesture, and the most he could manage, after dismissing the impulse, was to seek the solitude of his room, rushing back to the Bells' to escape all human contact. He knew he could never share with Hamish, or even with Jennie, the true state of his soul, but he also knew that sooner or later he would need human companionship, and that those two good folk would be the easiest with whom to be.

And so it was. Shortly after Hamish and Jennie returned, there was a discreet knock on Jamie's door, and there was Jennie with a cup of tea that almost spilled on them both, for all of a sudden Jamie was in her arms, sobbing out a grief he could not explain.

Jennie intuited that the tears were also related to Annie, although she did not know Annie, or even about Annie. Jamie's return to Erinsay could only mean, she had reasoned when the cryptic letter came, that all was not well on the mainland and that the healing was not yet done. And in this, Jennie's intuitions were clearer than Jamie's knowledge, for Jamie had thought that his problem could be solved by running from it and seeking refuge in the past, and that was not a thought that Jennie Bell could have entertained.

Jamie's tears released in Jennie the ability to cry as well, which she needed to do and had not been able to do. And so they held one another, and in their individual weaknesses made each other strong.

When eyes were dry, there was the quick cup of tea, it being late in the day and supper not far off. Hamish's grace at the evening meal almost brought Jamie to tears again, touching deep chords of which he had been unaware. For what Hamish prayed was, "O Lord, we give thee thanks for the life of Duncan MacDuff, and we grieve his departure from us. And we give thee thanks for the life of Jamie Stuart and we rejoice in his return to us . . ."—all of that, brand new, before getting onto familiar and manageable terrain: "For what we are about to receive, good Lord, make us truly thankful. Amen."

After the meal there was quiet talk around the fire. Duncan had died three nights earlier, part way through a tall tale in the pub, just like that. One moment he was standing in the middle of the floor, a group gathered around him, evoking laughter and drawing them all into a rollicking account of a mainland adventure in his youth in which poaching promised to play a leading role, and the next moment he was on the floor dead beyond all doubting of it. Nobody could remember whether he had had a heart condition or not. All they knew was that he would not finish the tale.

And though death was always a reality on the island, never shielded as so often it is on the mainland, the suddenness of it had affected them all. There was simply no way to imagine Duncan MacDuff dead. He had been thought indestructible. So much Hamish reported.

And Jamie?

Guardedly, he told them that there had not been a satisfactory resolution with his girl, and that he had felt the need to return to Erinsay. But now that he was finally here, he went on even more guardedly, he wasn't sure why he had come, especially in the light of Duncan's death, which (he said with massive understatement) had affected him deeply. He did not know what he was going to do, but he would like to stay for a while and figure out some next steps. He would pay two or three weeks' rent in advance and then see.

About to go upstairs again, he remembered that his gear was still in the sailboat. The three of them transported his remaining worldly goods in one easy trip.

"You travel powerful light, Jamie lad," was Hamish's comment. To which Jamie's unspoken rejoinder was, "When you're going where I intended to go, and you don't intend to return, you can afford to travel light, for there's nothing to take with you but yourself."

Going to the ceilidh had been Hamish's idea. After all, it was not just an ordinary evening of singing, recitations, and musical performance by the inhabitants of the village. Folk from the Other Side of the island would be coming over as well, and it would be "a rousing time all around," Hamish promised—not only the evening itself with all the music and speeches, but the day before and the day after would provide occasions for further festivity before everybody battened down for the long, gray winter. And Hamish hoped some of the mood might rub off on Jamie, who, by the look of him these days, could use all the help he could get. Hamish even proposed that Jamie, as a sometime resident of the manse, enter the ceilidh himself, doing a reading or singing, a suggestion Jamie instantly vetoed.

At most ceilidhs, while there is a spirit of friendly rivalry, the event is not so much to reward the participants as to encourage many folks to participate, no matter how competent or incompetent they seem to be. But for the upcoming event, it had already been announced that there were to be prizes as well, to encourage a few more souls who were willing to put themselves on the line in a brief competition. Indeed, there was already talk of an annual award, to be called the Duncan MacDuff Award, to be shared among the most outstanding participants from both sides of the island.

Coming so soon after the death of Duncan MacDuff, this

particular ceilidh was bound to have an edge of somberness, but no one seriously suggested a postponement, for everyone knew that Duncan would have been at the center of activity and would have played his pipes in the competition, a sure winner as always. Indeed, there were a couple of younger aspirants to the pipes who realized, in a mixture of sorrow and anticipation, that this ceilidh would be their first opportunity to emerge from the shadow of an acknowledged master and perform in their own right. The glens and hillsides echoed with the strains of their furious preparation.

Although nothing was scheduled to begin until eight o'clock, children were beginning to gather in the kirk hall by half past five on the day itself, scrambling for seats in the first two rows, and then fighting for their repossession after the inevitable trips to the lavatory in the long interval before the program began.

Certain places were reserved by custom. Everybody knew that the laird and his family would arrive about five minutes before the scheduled opening and be deferentially escorted to seats saved for them in the third row center. The three judges would be placed on the stage, over to one side; Hamish and Jennie would have aisle seats to the right, since it was, after all, the kirk hall, and toward the pastor of the kirk itself certain courtesies were always observed on such occasions. Jamie declined an invitation to join them in such a place of honor, feeling correctly that he had been no part of the custom's original intent, and told them, during Jennie's splendid high tea preceding the evening's program, that he would make his way to the hall on his own.

He did so, but badly miscalculated his timing, arriving so close to the opening number that the only possible place to sit was in very cramped quarters far to the back in a corner, squashed behind a pillar that made it virtually impossible for him to see the stage. Island time, Jamie realized too late, might be casual about most things, but it was rigid when ceilidhs were involved.

Tom Rutledge was the master of ceremonies, a role for which he had not been cast either by nature or providence, being more at home behind a plow or milking in the barn than standing on a stage joining subjects and predicates. So, after clearing his throat nervously while a hush settled over the audience, he confined his introductory remarks to announcing the name of the performer and the title of each piece, varying the order of events so that the telling of stories was interspersed with singing and piano playing.

All pieces were vigorously applauded, each act of acclaim being initiated and prolonged by members of the performer's own family, who usually sat *en bloc*; and sought by the degree of their enthusiasm to tip the estimate of the judges in the direction of their own sons, daughters, cousins, nieces, or nephews.

Alicia McLeod, after a false start triggered by nervousness, did a creditable rendition of the "Skye Boat Song." Tammas McBride and Jamie Fraser electrified the house with a dashing presentation of "Twa Heids," and Dominie Murchison, the schoolteacher, for whom the hall was darkened, told a tale of ghosts that had the children in the first two rows quiet, wide-eyed, and nonsquirming, until the denouement finally permitted squeals of suppressed terror to be exhaled in relief, and prompted half a dozen exits to the lavatory. Four lads from the Other Side of the island sang "Ye Banks and Braes of Bonnie Doon," and Jeannie Duff gave a recitation of Burns's "To a Field Mouse." The two pipers were placed back to back on the program, each visibly perspiring with nervousness, not only at the thought that comparisons with Duncan MacDuff were inevitable, but also at the thought that one of them would emerge heir-apparent over the other. As a result, both tried pieces considerably beyond their talents. Nevertheless, within a kirk hall, bagpipes are bagpipes, and the close confines made subtle discriminations so difficult that both were wildly applauded. A young woman whose name Jamie did not catch played "*Für Elise*," by Ludwig van Beethoven, the pronunciation of which gave Tom Rutledge a good deal of trouble with almost every word.

After more of the same, Jamie began to realize that the charm of a ceilidh resided not so much in the originality of the pieces as in the fact that they were being performed by friends and relatives. And since his friends on the island were few and his relatives were nil, his attention began to wander, and the increasing heat of the hall induced an ongoing and losing battle with somnolence. He had, in fact, just nodded off, when he heard, as from a distance, a last name that sounded like McCallum, and Tom Rutledge was finishing an announcement that sounded as though it contained a reference to the nearby isle of Eriskay.

A woman's voice, unaccompanied, filled the hall from the very first words, even though they were sung softly: "*Vair me o, o ro van o . . .*"

What can be said of her voice, save that it was clear and pure, and that when she sang the chorus, and came to "*Vair me o, o ru o ho*," she soared up to its high notes like a gull rising on a warm draft of air, with no outward motion, effortlessly, freely, cleanly?

There could be no mistaking. It was the voice of Moragh. Jamie leaned to the right to see around the pillar toward the center of the stage where she was standing, encountering an unyielding human shoulder that not only refused to give way, but sought to regain territory it felt was being unfairly challenged. Jamie shortly gave up shoulder wrestling as a distraction, and resigned himself to hearing and not seeing. Indeed, part of him acknowledged that he did not want to see the singer. It would be too painful to hear those words coming from a face that was not her face, even though the voice was her voice. So he closed his eyes, from which tears were almost escaping, and surrendered to memories of that first morning when Moragh McPherson had sung it in the kitchen by herself and it had been a memorial to Angus, and of that last evening when they had sung it together and it had been a betrothal song.

It was not hard to conjure up those memories since the voice was the same voice. Was he dreaming, even in the midst of his attentive listening? Was there even more mystery on this island than he had realized? If he had once gone backward in time, had Moragh now come forward in time? Was it some kind of trick? A blessed or cruel trick?

During the applause he addressed the owner of the unyielding shoulder: "Who was that who sang just now?"

"Eh?" was unyielding shoulder's response.

"The woman who just sang. What was her name?"

"Eh? Well now," came the response with all deliberate speed, "let me think on that. . . . That would be . . . ah, yes, that would be . . . the McCallum lass from Blairgowrie farm . . . on the other side of the island," he added, as Jamie appeared uncomprehending. "Lovely voice," the owner of the unyielding shoulder added gratuitously, in a burst of cordiality that left Jamie speechless, able only to nod in vigorous assent.

Taking the nod as conversational response of a high order, unyielding shoulder continued. "The McCallums have been farming Blairgowrie nigh on a hundred years now. Back then, there were a lot of sons and not so many daughters on the other side of the island, so a couple of the sons came over here a-courting, as plain as that, and one of them took back a granddaughter of old Tammas McPherson, and that's been a main thing holding the two sides of the island together ever since, the families being joined together, as you might say."

Tammas McPherson . . . wee Tammas? Yes, in time even wee Tammas would have been a grandfather.

The new information, far from satisfying Jamie, left him in need of still more, but the next event was already underway, and several minutes of a warbly tenor solo, with piano accompaniment, had to be endured before the conversation could be renewed.

During the round of applause, Jamie pursued: "That McCallum lass, would you be remembering her Christian name?"

"Eh?"

". . . her Christian name. The McCallum lass that sang a few minutes ago."

"Ah," unyielding shoulder shifted position. "Her Christian name . . ." He reflected at great length, obviously considering and then rejecting any number of alternatives. Finally, "No, I'd not be remembering."

He was settling back, the conversation satisfactorily concluded, when something in the intensity of Jamie's demeanor told him that the conversation was not satisfactorily concluded. So he turned to the woman on his right, addressed Jamie's question to her, received a response Jamie could not hear, inquired after her cousin on the mainland, exchanged opinions with her on the chances for rain within the evening, and turned back toward Jamie just as the choir from the kirk started a rendition of the metrical version of Psalm 139, one of the longer psalms. Only when the piece was finished, and the crowd had had enough sensibility not to applaud but to respond with reverential silence, did unyielding shoulder turn back to Jamie.

"Was it the McCallum lass you were asking about?" he queried, as from a great distance.

And after Jamie's nod of affirmation, "Her name be Moragh."

Coincidence, Jamie decided, but only after his heart had skipped several beats. Nevertheless, knowing the voice, he must see the face. He began craning around to see if he could spot Moragh among the contestants. Unyielding shoulder, although willing to have his conversational world invaded, remained consistently unwilling to yield an inch of physical space, and Jamie was firmly prohibited from extending his gaze.

"Ah, now," unyielding shoulder volunteered, after several more selections, as if to make clear that he bore no grudge, "it's the prizes they'll be announcing next."

"Excuse me," said Jamie, getting up and stepping across the space occupied by unyielding shoulder and his companion. He moved to a standing position in the aisle at the rear of the hall, which commanded a clear view of the stage, just in case a prize should be awarded to one Moragh McCallum.

Unyielding shoulder was right. It was on to the prizes. To no one's astonishment, Ian Kidd was awarded first prize for the intricate theme and variations he had rendered on his massive accordian, at which news the sixth row broke into cheers, whistles, and shouts of robust approbation, as a solid phalanx of Kidds acknowledged their familial hero. In a decision worthy of Solomon himself, second prize was divided equally between the two bagpipers, a judicious action that affirmed the remembered uniqueness of the late Duncan MacDuff, who would never have been awarded less than first prize. The action also indicated that no clear heir apparent had yet appeared on the scene, and ensured that both contestants would continue intense practicing until the next ceilidh came along.

After Tom Rutledge had dropped the folded sheet of paper sent up by the judges for the third award, kicked it halfway under the piano in an effort to retrieve it, kneeled over to pick it up, gotten dust on his hands which he ceremoniously removed with an enormous handkerchief, he ceremoniously cleared his throat and announced, "Third prize to Moragh McCallum, for her rendition of . . ." The rest of the announcement was lost in the applause initiated by the group of McCallums and their friends midway back in the hall, who had come over as one from the Other Side of the island.

A form arose from among the celebrating entourage, mounted the steps and turned, blushing, to receive a further accolade from the full audience and a small envelope from the hand of Tom Rutledge.

But Jamie was not looking at the transfer of a small envelope. He was looking at a face. He had been told that it was the face of Moragh McCallum. But it was the face of Moragh McPherson.

In the social time afterward, he got as close to Moragh McCallum as he dared, and her gaze went past him, all uncomprehending.

It was a confused Jamie who returned to the manse that

night. Was there still a magic on the island? Was there a coming together of time past and time present? Where was "real" time? Was it the time he was now in, and did that mean that the past time with Moragh McPherson was not real? Or was it in the time back then, so that the time he was now in was a sort of dream? Could he be in a dream and know it was a dream? Could he dream he was having a dream?

Moragh was in both times. Or were there two Moraghs? Had the earlier Moragh come back to him now, having escaped from the fire as he did, in some warp of time? Or was the present Moragh simply a distant descendant of the one he had known, the contrivance of a genetic trick in whom, five generations later there had been reproduced another who seemed precisely the one to whom he had pledged his love and the one who had pledged her love in return?

After a night punctuated this time by sleeplessness rather than nightmares, as well as by a driving rain that beat upon the roof and left him even more agitated, Jamie resolved that he must get over to the Other Side of the island and meet Moragh McCallum, who was either his own Moragh about to be returned to him if he could only find the key to unlock her memory, or one so like her that he was already more than half in love with her.

While he was turning these matters over, Callum the Post drove up, got out of the Royal Mail van, and ambled up to the door of the manse to leave the post and have a cup of tea in the kitchen with Jennie, where he tried, unsuccessfully, to ferret out of that honorable and discreet woman some items of interest that he could relay to others at his subsequent stops.

Callum's twice-weekly rounds obviated the need for a local newspaper on Erinsay. He was the modern equivalent of the *seannachie*, the teller of tales, who used to go from village to

village and door to door in the old days, relaying news, information, and gossip. Callum had enough discretion not to pur-
vey gossip, so he was well trusted. But since Jennie's
information, garnered usually from sick beds, was often of a
particularly private sort, she exercised what she thought of as
"the seal of the confessional." Hot irons themselves could not
have extracted from her words that had been spoken in trust,
and not even Hamish was allowed to share them save in ways
that would never betray their speaker. So as Callum left, fifteen
minutes later, he realized that although he was scarcely more
informed than when he had arrived, Jennie Bell's knowledge
of island news had probably been amplified at least fourfold.

"So it's off to the Other Side I'll be, Jennie, and thank you
kindly for the tea," Jamie heard Callum say as he left the
house. "It's not an easy trip after the night's rain on the Rutted Road, or for sure I'd stay for a second cup."

"Callum!" Jamie thought. "That's my way to the McCallum
farm to meet Moragh. By the sound of their names, he's a rel-
ative and will go in for another cup of tea." Hurriedly tying his
shoes, Jamie raced down the stairs to catch up with the Royal
Mail and see if a passenger who had a curiosity about visiting
the Other Side of the island could be accommodated in the
front of the van.

But Callum's speed behind the steering wheel was considerably greater than his speed in entering and leaving a house,
and by the time Jamie had made it to the porch he was gone.
Jamie realized that Callum's next trip would not be for a full
three days, which would give him time to contrive a way of
going along, though he spent most of it restlessly struggling
not only with the puzzle of the two Moraghs—or the one Moragh, as might indeed be the case in such a place as Erinsay—
but also with an increasingly single-minded attachment to

Moragh McCallum, whoever, in the riddle of time, she might turn out to be.

Two nights later at the pub Jamie contrived to sit by Callum and buy him a drink. Did Callum go to the Other Side of the island on every delivery of the post?

"Aye."

Did he ever take a passenger along?

"For what would a body want to ride the Royal Mail?"

Suppose one simply wanted to see other parts of the island?

"Aye, it would make good sense to do so."

Did he often take passengers with him on the Royal Mail?

"Nay."

Was he allowed to do it?

"It's not the custom . . ."

But?

". . . it has been done."

Could it be done tomorrow?

"It is not clear."

Why not?

"Suppose there's a huge pile of mail that fills the other seat."

Agreed. But suppose there were room?

"It could be done."

Was there a charge?

"There's no *official* charge" (with just the slightest hint of an emphasis on the word "official").

Jamie got what he felt was the message: Would Callum like another pint?

"I'd not be turning it down."

A long pause while the pint was savored. Then pursuit continued. So someone could go tomorrow?

"It is possible. Provided, of course . . ."

Provided what?

"Provided, as was said before, there's not too many packets from the steamer."

Of course.

"But who, may I ask, would be wanting to ride the Royal Mail?"

Perhaps Jamie himself.

"Well, now, in that case, I'll see you at the manse a wee bit past ten."

Splendid.

"And there's no official charge, you understand?"

Jamie understood. Would Callum like another pint?

"I'd not be turning it down."

Having estimated by this conversation, the nature of Callum's dialogical exchanges, Jamie resigned himself to the likelihood that a mainlander like himself was liable to extract little information from Callum about the McCallums during the dispatching of the Royal Mail.

The morning proved him correct. Callum's reputation for relaying interesting information was limited to those whose habitation on the island was year-round.

As they stopped at the various farms, Jamie would be left in the cab of the Royal Mail as Callum made his leisurely information-gathering rounds. Jamie was thus in a frenzy of anxiety after they had traversed the Rutted Road and a stop was finally made at the McCallums' farm—the identification of which he divined from the packet of mail the postman picked up with that name on top.

Callum swung out of the cab with a grace bestowed on him

by years of practice, and ambled up the path to the kitchen door of the house. He knocked and entered without waiting for a response, a sure indication, Jamie decided, of blood relationship. The door closed. Jamie fumed at his ineptitude in having been excluded from the one room on the entire island to which it was imperative that he gain access. He examined the piles of assorted mail still left in the cab, desperately hoping to find a stray piece marked "McCallum" so that in an act of great helpfulness he could take it up to the house. He found none.

Would it be indecorous, he wondered, for a stranger simply to go to the door, knock, and request use of "the facilities?" Surely when he emerged they would ask him to stay for a cup of tea. Besides, his anxiety was making such a request more and more imperative.

Just as he was about to resort to this stratagem, the door of the farmhouse opened and Callum started walking back to the Royal Mail. But he stopped after a couple of steps, waved to Jamie, and shouted, "We're a wee bit ahead of schedule today in spite of the rain, so the mistress says to stay for a cup of tea. You're free to join us, if you like."

Back over the mountain and down the Rutted Road at last, Jamie asked Callum to let him off the van so he could walk the rest of the way, "and stretch the legs," as he put it. But it was the mind and spirit of Jamie Stuart that wanted stretching, for they had become cramped beyond all containment in the tiny cab of the postal van.

It had been Moragh, all right, his own Moragh! Though reborn generations later in another body, she was as like her great-great-great-great-great grandmother as though she were a twin.

This Moragh, of course, was younger than the Moragh he

had known. There were no lines of care across the fresh, young face. Not to be wondered at: she had not, after all, borne two sons and brought them through a dozen years, nor endured the loss of a husband and a daughter, nor settled into the dreary prospect of forty or fifty years in solitude without the warm embrace of a man. But she was all that his own Moragh had been. With joy, he remembered that he had been able to intuit her responses through that teatime, to know in advance how she would tilt her head, how she would pour the tea, even the way she had straightened her back and brought her hands together, prior to getting up and signaling that teatime was over and the men had best be on their way so she and her mother could get to work preparing the evening meal.

As he walked along, his heart sang—for the first time in many months—with the possibility of a broken love restored. For although she had met him only once, he had met her many times. Ah, what had back then been terminated rudely, abruptly, horribly, would now be fulfilled lovingly, completely, tenderly.

He came to a road leading up one of the valleys, and remembered visiting a farm there, early in his first stay on the island, when he was trying to find the path to the Faery Glen. And suddenly, out of the deep recesses of memory, stored there and forgotten, words worked their way to the surface of his consciousness. What was it Jane Darley's mother had said, the woman who (so her daughter had reported) had the gift of the second sight?

Two loves you'll have . . .

That much came back easily. And then there had been a part about

. . . with names alike . . .

But what else? What else? It had seemed so incongruous at the time that he had dismissed the words and failed to take the episode as a whole seriously. ". . . With names alike . . ." he repeated to himself. What beyond that?

And then the gears of memory meshed and spun out the words:

> . . . in different parts of time.

He reported aloud:

> Two loves you'll have
> With names alike
> In different parts of time.

Who could doubt the wisdom of those possessing the second sight? He arrived at the manse ravenously hungry for the first time in many weeks.

Two days later, Jamie Stuart, rucksack loaded with provisions for both lunch and tea, and field glasses handy to watch the birds (his public explanation for the outing), set out toward the Rutted Road.

By the time he had passed the road to the Faery Glen, he had already improved on the words he had heard from the woman with the second sight. "One love I have," was the song he now sang, "and her name is the same, in every part of time."

And *Vair me o* he sang as well, this time to a new Moragh: "Thou'rt the music of my heart, harp of joy, *o cruit mo chridh*," remembering that the Gaelic meant "harp of my heart." He sang softly at first and then triumphantly aloud, to the surprise and discomfiture of a nearby flock of sheep who, upon hearing the boisterous tenor voice, scattered in all directions, adding their voices to the song.

At the top of the Rutted Road he stopped to eat at a look-out well up the slope of Ben Erinsay. To the west he could see the sea, from which the gentle sloping pastures made their way to where he was sitting, while behind him was the rockier terrain of the east of Erinsay, and the hills of Ben Moire and Ben Essie between him and the mainland, with the Cuillins in and out of view. The sun was bright and the sky was blue. The sea was emerald green above the sands, and deep blue and purple where the kelp and seaweed floated near the surface. With his glasses he spotted not only birds but seals, sleek and fat as they sunned themselves on the rocks. Here and there the coves that surrounded the glistening white beaches were visible even from the heights.

Refreshed by his sandwiches and coffee, and saving a thermos of tea, a packet of water biscuits, and a bar of chocolate for later in the day, he started down the gentle westward slope, past the first farms, and finally about the middle of the afternoon arrived at the kitchen door of the McCallum farm. He would do no formal speechmaking today. All that he hoped would happen was that some deeper bonds of acquaintance and the beginnings of friendship might be established, laying the groundwork for the "courting" that in the rhythm of island custom would have to be slow and deliberate.

She answered his knock, was momentarily disconcerted by the presence of an apparent stranger, searched her memory to place him, and then as her face cleared, opened the door yet wider.

"Ah, Mr. Stuart it is," she said with a smile of recognition. "Do come in. We're glad to welcome you once again. You'll be having a cup of tea with us, I imagine?" And she moved toward the stove to push the kettle to a spot that would bring the already heated water to a boil.

Conversation was easy as she moved around the kitchen, putting some scones on the oven to warm, opening the crock that held a supply of already baked pancakes, scooping jam from a container onto a large plate and cutting a slab of butter from a small tub.

"Please don't trouble yourself," Jamie said, in the wake of such preparation.

"Ah, 'tis no trouble at all. My mother will be joining us in a moment for her tea as well."

The announcement forced Jamie to adjust his conversational timetable.

"I was just walking by," he pursued hastily, "and I wanted to tell you again how much I enjoyed your singing at the ceilidh."

"Ah, you're far too kind, Mr. Stuart," she said, blushing. "But it's a beautiful song I've always loved. It came from Eriskay up to the north, but we've made it our own here on the island for many generations. I learned it from my grandmother, and she from her mother, and so on. They all had the same name I have, so it's a song I've always felt was part of me."

"I love it too," Jamie replied. "It's as if I'd known it for a hundred years." And then, though only to himself, "As I have, and that's for sure."

And then, out loud again: "When I heard you sing, and when I met you here the other day, it was as though I'd always known you."

"Why thank you, Mr. Stuart," she replied in full innocence. "We hope to make folk feel welcome here. I'm glad you wanted to return."

And then, just as Jamie was about to engage in a quantum

conversational leap based on her response, there was an unexpected entrance. It was not the mother from the living room, but someone else from the outside entrance near the barn.

Turning at the sound of the opening door, Moragh's face went all alight. "Ah, Donald," she cried, "how good you could come so early. I wasn't expecting you for sure till after teatime."

And he, moving toward her all eagerly, saying "Moragh . . . ," stopped full in his tracks, embarrassed, when he saw Jamie. Jamie had a sinking feeling that but for his own presence this interloper might have embraced the woman standing between them.

Moragh, sensing that they did not know each other, intervened promptly.

"Ah, forgive me, Mr. Stuart. This is Donald Kibbie. Donald, this is Mr. Stuart from the mainland, who has been having a holiday on the island."

"It's a pleasure to meet you, Mr. Stuart." Donald extended a strong, calloused hand. "And if I'm not mistaken, I saw you many weeks ago at the pub, on a night when Duncan MacDuff was having a go at the pipes."

After suitable recognition by all that it was easier for an islander to remember the face of one stranger than for a stranger to remember the faces of all the islanders, Moragh felt that some further information needed to be imparted. Turning to Jamie, she explained, "Donald is a shepherd on the nearby croft who sometimes helps my father." After a very slight pause she continued, "We've been keeping company these two years, and," her face bursting with joy and love, "we're to be married Saturday week in the kirk."

Donald, not to be outdone in radiating cordiality, added,

"And Mr. Stuart, sir, if you're still on the island at that time, I do hope you'll do us so great an honor as to attend our wedding."

When the tea was poured, Jamie found himself seated by old Mrs. McCallum, who was garrulous and slightly hard of hearing, so that the conversation was mostly one-sided. It was the only kind of conversation Jamie Stuart could have handled at that point. He learned as much as he cared to learn about the glories of living on the west side of the island, and considerably more than he cared to learn about the virtues of Mrs. McCallum's future son-in-law. He learned that Donald was about to drive a herd of a thousand sheep over the mountains and down the Rutted Road to the east harbor so that he could ferry them in stages by sheep barge to Oban, where a sale had been arranged. He learned that the proceeds of the sale would provide a nest egg for Donald and Moragh to set up housekeeping after the wedding. He learned that Donald could not swim—a condition curiously widespread among a large proportion of the male population of Erinsay—and fervently hoped that he would fall into the nearest watering trough. He learned how thoughtful and generous Donald was, and that if Donald was lucky to have won Moragh (a self-evident truth to both Mrs. McCallum and her reluctant listener), so too was Moragh fortunate in casting her lot with Donald, a tribute that seemed to Jamie uncommonly handsome on the lips of a future mother-in-law.

Throughout these and other encomiums, Moragh and Donald were separated from the others and fully satisfied with one another's company, even if neither one had the facility to say so directly with words. But an occasional touch of hands under the table, that Jamie could intuit if not empirically confirm, intensified their communal joy and his solitary misery.

Wretched, he took his leave as soon as he could without seeming to deprecate the island hospitality that had been extended to an almost total stranger. Conscious of hypocrisy, he wished Donald and Moragh a long and happy marriage, and stumbled down the path to the road.

He walked rapidly and furiously up the gentle slope from the west, never looking back until, winded, he stopped at the foot of Ben Erinsay before beginning the more tortuous descent on the other side.

The tea in the thermos was no longer piping hot, and he poured it out on the ground in a rage. The chocolate was slightly moldy. The water biscuits, living up to their name, were soggy. Such outer realities only reflected his inner mood. Once again to have come so close to the fulfillment of a dream, and to have had that dream denied so rudely, so abruptly, so destructively . . . He was unable to articulate either his rage or his hurt. The hurt was deeper than the rage, and therefore harder to acknowledge, so he nursed the rage and contented himself with cursing a God in whom he scarcely believed, and whose hidden visage he could discern only as a frown.

The universe itself seemed intent on frustrating, if not destroying, him, for even as he sat on a large rock, the sky clouded over, and a sudden squall drenched him. It seemed a baptism into death rather than life. And then, as suddenly as the storm had risen, it abated, and by the time he was halfway down the Rutted Road, he was dry once again, save for his socks and shoes, and the sky was an incredible blue, as blue as it had been in the morning. Only this time, instead of fortifying him, it mocked him.

Late that evening and through most of the night, Jamie Stuart struggled. Where did this turn of events leave him? Was he, once again, simply too late? Should he passively accept this new state of affairs or should he fight? And if so, with what conceivable weapons? After quickly and commendably ruling out the murder of Donald Kibbie as a solution, he moved on to more realistic possibilities.

He could "tell Moragh all," and indicate his legitimate claim upon her affections. But he realized, almost as soon as he formulated his case, the predictable ineffectiveness of an argument beginning with the words, "I was in love with your great-great-great-great-great-grandmother, and you are exactly like her, so I love you too."

He could return to Moragh and, without reference to the past, simply make his case: "I have fallen instantly and irrevocably in love with you. I knew it the first time I heard your voice, even more the first time I saw you, and now that I have met you, I cannot contain my love for you."

And then he replayed the scene from Morage's perspective: a man she had known for half an hour, who was a good ten years older than she, was asking her to forsake at the last minute a courtship that had been two years in the making with a man with whom she was manifestly in love, and to set aside custom and expectation on the part of all her friends of a lifetime. He could almost hear the words of an earlier Moragh— "Oh, Jamie, it wouldn't be fitting"—and realized that he could not handle even the hint of such a response on the lips of the present Moragh.

He could remain on the island and be supportive of Moragh and Donald, grandly accepting Donald's invitation to remain for the wedding. It would be his abdication of all claims, his offering up of his own frustrated love for the sake of Moragh's future. It appealed to a strain in him both noble and masochistic. He knew he could never pull it off.

He could pack his few belongings and leave the island for good. No one knew his secret, no one would question his departure, no one (he reflected ruefully) would really miss him, except perhaps Hamish and Jennie. It was the only alternative left. He would make one last ritual visit to his various haunts, explore with particular care the ruins near a certain green mound, and then be off the island forever.

But he had just given Jennie another week's rent, and he realized that an earlier departure than that would cause raised eyebrows on that rugged and honest face, a face before which, even in his misery, he did not care to dissimulate. A week it was.

Vair me o permeated his dreams that night, particularly the last line of the refrain, "Sad am I without thee." In his troubled sleep the music had irreversibly recast itself in a minor key, more plaintive and haunting than ever. No effort of his semi-conscious mind could get it back into the major key in which it had been written. But, as he reflected on waking, major or minor, the words remained the same, "Sad am I without thee."

When light broke upon the island and brought him to full consciousness, they remained as an epitaph. The most he could salvage was that for a time the words had meant "Happy am I *with* thee." But no promises were attached.

Jamie was sitting out the storm in the Bell's living room, trying to get a weather report on the Home Service which was being intermittently drowned out by static. He was awed by the swiftness with which nature could change on the islands from a beneficent to a despotic force. In the early morning hours the sea had been calm; Donald and his friend Murdo, with Moragh's help, had loaded the sheep barge with the last load of sheep, and the two of them had taken off, planning to complete the final return trip before the long, bright evening had ended. Moragh had stayed on the island and had gone around with Jennie to see some relatives and firm up the last-minute plans for the wedding.

Jamie, unable to cope with the immediacy of Moragh's presence, had fled the manse on a hike, but the fury of the sudden afternoon storm had forced him back into the protective arms of the house. Before turning on the wireless, he had sensed a restlessness in Hamish which so filled the room that he finally decided he had no alternative but to probe it.

"Hamish, you're full of worry by the look of things. What is it, man? You're driving me daft with your pacing, and your getting up, and your sitting down."

Relief at being able to share the tension took the edge off Hamish's anxiety for a second. "Jamie," he responded, "we got a phone call just an hour ago from Murdo on the far island. You know, of course, that Murdo is not one to use a telephone except in the most dire of emergencies. Well, the last load made it safely over with the sheep, and the buyer was there, and the transfer was completed, and Donald has the money in hand, all of which will be good news to Moragh. We relaxed.

"But Murdo decided to stay over with some friends, and it being so fair a day just a few hours back, Donald decided to sail the sheep barge back alone. And now, of course, since Donald knows little about how to handle the barge save in clear weather, and a fierce gale now has whipped up, Murdo is worried about his friend. And so am I, for unless he read the weather warnings in the sky and took refuge in some cove, Donald is out in that storm right now . . ."

Hamish looked out the window, where the trees were struggling with the wind, shivered, and turned his glance inside again.

". . . Out there in that tub of a boat, and him not knowing how to swim. Moragh will be wild with fear when she and Jennie return, and I'm duty-bound to tell her there's not a thing we can do from here but watch from the harbor and pray, and to Moragh that will hardly seem enough."

Donald Kibbie and Angus McPherson were for a moment juxtaposed in Jamie's imagination. Did the sea have some cruel need to destroy the companions of those named Moragh? He shook himself clear of the vision, for Moragh and Jennie could be seen coming up the front walk, holding on to each other, their bodies bent forward against the torrential lash of wind and rain.

Involvement in the pastoral crisis about to ensue was more than Jamie cared for, so he walked quickly to the kitchen and put on his slicker, preparing to go out the back door and down to the pier. He assumed, rightly, that a large part of the population would have gathered there in spite of the weather to watch for any sight of the sheep barge. He took for granted that the information Hamish had just communicated to him was now known throughout the island, especially since it had come in over an open trunk line.

But he did not escape the house that easily. Moragh burst in as he was about to leave, panic on her face, having just heard the news from Hamish. "Mr. Stuart," she managed to ask through a succession of short breaths, "will Donald be safe? You know the sea. The pastor says you sailed here yourself from the mainland. Is it safe for Donald? What can we do? What can we do?"

In Moragh's face Jamie saw the face of another Moragh as she looked when she used to dwell on the death of Angus. The images of the two faces fused into one. He could not separate them, no matter how hard he tried.

"I don't know, lass," he responded a few seconds later, speaking to them both, "but I'll just be running down to the pier to see what can be done."

The rain stopped as suddenly as it had begun, but the wind was, if anything, more fierce than before. Jamie headed first for the summit of The Rise, where he knew he could see a farther horizon than would be possible at the pier. As he arrived breathless at the top, he thought he saw something in the wild gray water far beyond the pier, hidden from the sight of those below. Reaching around awkwardly into the rucksack on his back, Jamie pulled out the field glasses he always carried with him for bird watching, and stopping for a moment, he focused them on the horizon. Just in view was a sheep barge, very low in the water, obviously in danger of foundering. Within it was someone who could only be presumed to be Donald Kibbie, bending over an engine that could only be presumed to have ceased functioning.

In the time it took Jamie to lower the field glasses and return them to his rucksack, a mixture of wildly contrary reactions had surged through him, all commanding simultaneous attention.

He recognized immediately that if no one got there to rescue him, Donald Kibbie would almost surely drown. An ugly prospect.

He recognized almost as immediately that if that happened, he, Jamie Stuart, would then be free to court and possibly win the hand of Moragh McCallum. An attractive prospect.

He remembered, simultaneously, the look of anguish on Moragh McCallum's face just moments ago, and realized with unambiguous clarity that if ever he were in a position to court and possibly win Moragh McCallum, it could only be in the sure knowledge that he had done everything possible to save Donald Kibbie. Under no other circumstances could he ever look Moragh McCallum full in the face, or remember the face of Moragh McPherson, without shame.

He knew without knowing how or why he knew it, that if he truly loved Moragh McCallum, he must desire for her what *she* most desired, and he also knew that what she most desired was the safe return of Donald Kibbie. That, then, must be his own intent. Never before had anything seemed so clear and so clean . . . and so devastating.

What it came down to was this: long ago on the night of a great fire, Moragh McPherson had risked—and given—her life for Jamie Stuart.

And now, partly as an act of gratitude for the gift, Jamie must risk *his* life as a healing for Moragh McCallum and her deep fear, on the day of a great storm. What he had received from one Moragh—the gift of life—he must try to make available to the other.

It was a fearful symmetry, but once he acknowledged it, his mind was clear: he must do whatever it would take to save the life of Donald Kibbie. It would be his gift to the two Moraghs.

Realizing that once he climbed down from The Rise, the sheep barge would be out of sight, and knowing that The Rise was visible from beyond the harbor, Jamie, with a navigator's instinct, located the sheep barge on a line between The Rise and a small peak on the furthermost island. He calculated that by sailing toward that peak on a line from The Rise he would be likely to spot the sheep barge, even allowing for considerable drift.

He ran back to the pier, trimmed the sail of his boat, declined offers of assistance, and embarked alone into the storm.

The one who could best tell what happened after that was Donald Kibbie. He was in shock when, on toward evening, Jamie's sailboat was thrust up on a beach a full two miles south of the harbor, its keel grinding into the sand and pitching Donald out into the shallow surf through which he crawled by instinct up beyond the high-tide line and fainted dead away.

It was old Jed Jedburgh who found him, at first thinking him dead, and half dragged, half carried him to his farm. The island's mystical communication system was working overtime, and Moragh McCallum found her way there within the hour.

Donald, terror in his face still, told Moragh enough so that later, when he had calmed down, he could talk to the men assembled there, and tell them what had happened over the horizon and just out of sight of the harbor where they had all been standing.

"For sure, the barge was shipping water fast, and I was cursing my stupidity in having started back across that stretch of open water alone, even though the day was fair and the sky was blue when I left. But soon the sky was gray and the wind was strong and the sea was most unfriendly. And I was foolish beyond all believing not to have made my way to some cove while I could still steer the barge. It was as though the Day of Judgment had come. The waves began to break into the barge, and I was sloshing around trying to bail it out, but the first thing I knew the motor had flooded out, and try as I would, I couldn't get it started.

"So now I was at the mercy of the wind and waves, and swearing at myself and heaven that I, who could not even swim, was out alone in a terrible storm and was about to die. And I thought of Moragh, and I was despairing and angry at myself, when all of a sudden, almost on top of me, I saw the sail of Mr. Stuart's boat, and there he was, waving at me and shouting, though over the wind I couldn't hear the words.

He skirted by, very fast, and then turned about to come past me again. And this time I saw he was waving a rope that was tied to his mast, and as he went by he threw the rope to me, with a life-preserver on the end, and I caught the rope as the life preserver skimmed past me, and held on tightly as it went through my hands, which as you can see are burned like sin, for I saw that I must hold the rope lest the life-preserver slip by me once again.

"And then I was out in the fearful water, holding on for dear life, but the waves were so high and my hands so raw that even holding on to the life-preserver I couldn't inch myself toward his boat. So Mr. Stuart let go of the tiller and began, arm over arm, to haul me in."

Donald paused, shutting his eyes as though to shut out the scene, though in reality he was trying to control tears that were born of fatigue and terror.

"It was hard work for him," Donald continued, "and more than once he had to duck the boom of that wild sail, and I don't know where he got the energy, but slowly he pulled me, flailing in the water like a three-year-old, toward the boat, and then, when I was at the side he reached over, grabbed my shoulders, pulled me up and over the side and dumped me in the bottom of the boat, exhausted, but with my eyes open now and able to see what was going on.

"And all the while the boat, with no one at the tiller, was careening around in that wild sea like a pain-crazed sheep. And as we went down the trough of one wave I could see over the side that the sheep barge was sinking out of sight, and I marveled that if I had still been on it I would have been sinking too. I tried to shout a 'thank you' to this man I scarcely knew, but I had no energy or breath to do anything but lie there, all of a heap, and count myself lucky to be alive at all.

"And then I saw a fearful thing . . ."

And here Donald, all man that he was, did break down, and Moragh had to comfort him in the midst of his shame that he, a grown man, was crying in the presence of other grown men, which is not a thing they do on the isles.

But when he had finished, for sure there was no man in the room with dry eyes, and they all, without a word being spoken, had acknowledged that there are some things to shed tears over, even though one will never say to another that the tears were shed.

For what Donald saw was this:

". . . Mr. Stuart, who had been leaning over the side to haul me in, turned around and lay there just a moment to get his wind back, before he started back to the tiller, so I saw his face and he saw mine. And there was a look of triumph in his eyes, and a look of fierce joy, and just as our eyes met in the boat and my eyes said 'thank you,' a fearful gust of wind caught the sail, and it swung around, and the boom caught him full force across the forehead, and where there had been that look of triumph there was only a huge gash and ready flow of blood, as he was pushed backward out of the boat and into that fearful sea.

"I tried to scream and move toward where he had been, but I could make no sound, and all went black on me. And the next thing I knew I was spilled out into the sea as well, only it was a gentler sea and my knees were on the bottom and I was crawling up the beach without scarcely knowing it and yelling 'Mr. Stuart, Mr. Stuart' like a madman.

"But there was no sound save the washing of the waves and the sobbing of my heart if I was alive and he was dead."

The sobbing of his heart took over again in the tiny farmhouse of Jed Jedburgh. And soon the strong men with no dry eyes filtered their way out. It seeming proper to do so, and soon no one was left to comfort him but Moragh. She placed his head in her lap, a more familiar gesture than they had ever shared before, the customs of the islands being what they are. And she stroked his hair and sobbed too, but hers was a sobbing of relief from a heavy burden of fear and sorrow and the sobbing of a still fearful joy that her man, whom she had thought dead, was alive again. And now and then, between her sobs, she could be heard whispering, "Thank you, thank you, Mr. Stuart." And then she sobbed for him as well, but it was sobbing of a different sort.

They found the body of Jamie Stuart at the beach called Traigh Siochail, which in the Gaelic means "the peaceful beach," or "a place of peace."

It was well named, that beach, for the sea had washed the bloody gash all clean, and for sure the face of Jamie Stuart was at last a face at peace.

After
Erinsay

There was no family to claim the body. And so, in accordance with the custom lingering from the two great wars, that those "washed up by the sea" be granted a final resting place on Erinsay, Jamie Stuart was buried in the newest section of the graveyard. He was the second to be laid there, Duncan MacDuff having preceded him by a few weeks only. His new stone was in marked contrast to an ancient one close by, on which those with keen eyes can still make out the legend: "Moragh McPherson . . . died by fire . . ."

There are *many* on the island who claim that on any night "above the wash of the waves, the song of the seals is heard, faint yet persistent, singing two alternating notes."

There are *some* on the island who claim that on Friday nights, if you listen intently, you can till hear the singing of the Wee Folk on the sitheans, the green mounds.

There are *a few* on the island who claim that if you are near the graveyard on certain Friday nights, you can hear, ever so faintly, the pipes of Duncan MacDuff, who rises from his grave long enough to do a skirl and summon those who hear to come and join the celebration.

And there are *a very few* on the island who claim that if you pass the graveyard on a certain Friday night each year when the pipes are playing, you can also see, rising from the adjoining graves, the forms of Moragh McPherson and Jamie Stuart, and that as long as the pipes are playing, they join in a dance both solemn and joyful, above the holy sod.

An Eriskay Love Lilt

Words & Music Kenneth MacLeod and Marjory Kennedy-Fraser